Quinn s[...]
as a sedu[...]

Nicole faced him angrily. "You don't know the first thing about me."

He laughed insolently, and caught her against him. "I wanted you from the first moment I saw you."

"But I might not want you," she claimed desperately. "You're hard and you're ruthless and you shun deep involvement. In a way you're afraid of it, and I'm certainly afraid of you. I don't want to be an object of desire, some idiot possession. I'm a person with needs and wants of my own."

"None of which has anything to do with me?" he countered. "Go on, put me straight."

The terrible part was she couldn't. She was hopelessly in love with him—and he wanted no part of her love.

White Magnolia

by

MARGARET WAY

Harlequin Books

TORONTO • LONDON • NEW YORK • AMSTERDAM
SYDNEY • HAMBURG • PARIS

Original hardcover edition published in 1979
by Mills & Boon Limited

ISBN 0-373-02276-X

Harlequin edition published August 1979

CHAPTER ONE

It had been a long, exhausting day, draining her frail energy to the last dregs. Even a shower and shampoo had failed to cool her throbbing body and the prickling of dust was still in her nostrils. Nicole bit her lip and her pale face held the expression of one very close to tears. The heat was blistering, the worst she had ever known.

Over her head, an ancient ceiling fan oscillated noisily and the light in the small hotel room was so bad, she had to walk to the dressing table and peer into the dismally spotted mirror to apply moisturiser to her thirsting skin. It glistened on the matt surface and lent it a pearlescent sheen. It struck her bleakly that she looked utterly incongruous in this rather shabby little room which, nevertheless, was acknowledged as the pub's best.

Every movement of her body, the bend of her classical dark head seemed imbued with melancholy. One had to be desperate to lose oneself in the scorching Outback, but then she *was* desperate, wasn't she? Did it matter if she confessed it to herself? Sadly, she sank down on to the small stool before the dressing table. One had to make one's own peace in life. Her world had changed, but she had no other course but to look to a future. The dim light outlined the pure curve of her cheek from brow to chin, the gleaming, curling dark cloud of hair, the large almond-shaped dark eyes, the delicate black brows, like wings. Her own beauty had never moved her as it moved others. It was simply there, inherited from the mother she had scarcely known.

The fan rattled loudly, but there was no delicious

breeze. She drew a deep breath, trying to calm her fluttering nerves. In the morning someone would come from Sapphire to collect her. Nothing was as bad as it seemed. She was overtired, that was it; hardly able to control her feelings or the acid bitterness of her memories. It was curiously like being ... haunted. She shuddered then, looking at her hands with dismay.

A rap at the door broke her immobility. She jumped to her feet and stood undecided, her heart contracting a little because she was wearing only her nightgown and matching peignoir.

'Miss Lindfield?'

Nicole closed her eyes in relief, then moved forward quickly. She opened the door and there was the plump, motherly figure of the proprietor's wife outlined against the stabbing light. She was carrying a tray and her eyes softened involuntarily in response to Nicole's appearance.

'What gorgeous clothes you wear! That would look wicked on me! Got a little nightcap for you, dear. I thought you might need it.'

'That's very kind of you, Mrs Gray!' Nicole stepped aside as the woman walked into the room.

'No bother, dear. Not used to the heat, are you? You were paper-white when you came in.'

'I expect I'll feel better in the morning.'

'I hope so, dear.' Mrs Gray put the tray down on the small bedside table. 'Be sure to pull the net now, or the mozzies will eat you alive.'

Nicole had already inspected the net and found it clean. 'Yes, I'll do that.'

Mrs Gray looked at her with the utmost admiration. 'Be sure to tell Mr Rossiter we did everything to make you welcome. You've got our best room.'

'Thank you.' Not for the world would Nicole have said

anything tactless, though the pain in her temples was increasing.

Despite her beauty and her poise Mrs Gray thought the girl looked ill. 'Hurry up and get into bed now. You're exhausted, that's the trouble. Mr Rossiter will be here in the morning to get you. How exciting to be staying with the family. They're very glamorous to the likes of us—all that money and land and Mr Rossiter is the most marvellous man!'

'I don't know him,' Nicole said in her lovely gentle voice.

'Really, dear?' Mrs Gray looked amazed. 'I thought everyone in this part of the world knew him, and you're going to visit the family. . . .'

'I went to university with Christine,' Nicole explained.

'Ah!' Mrs Gray stared at her quite frankly, fascinated by the delicate exoticism of the girl's appearance, the exquisite and probably wildly expensive nightwear. 'So it's your first visit. You're going to love it. Sapphire is a show place and Mr Rossiter is a very powerful man. The strong one, like his father and old Luke Rossiter before him. Sapphire is the biggest property in the whole of the South-West, and the family have managed to keep it intact. Quinn's grandfather was a wonderful old man. A hard man, mind, but a real character!' Mrs Gray crossed slowly to the door, then hesitated. 'What would you like for breakfast, dear?'

'Really, I don't bother.' Nicole stood trembling a little, disturbed by the thought of the large cooked breakfast Mrs Gray obviously envisaged.

'Must eat your breakfast, dear. You don't want to be airsick, do you?'

Common courtesy forced Nicole into her answer. 'Perhaps tea and toast when I get up. May I call you, Mrs Gray?'

'Certainly, dear, if you think that's enough. No wonder you're so light. Why, one of our willy-willies would blow you away.' She lifted her head in a pleasant gesture. 'Now I'll go away and leave you. You look all in. Goodnight, dear.'

'Goodnight, Mrs Gray.' Nicole roused herself and walked to the door to shut it. 'Thank you for the night-cap.'

'Be sure you drink it. It will help you to sleep.' Mrs Gray's kind, plump face creased into another smile. 'Would you like me to call you in the morning?'

'No, it's all right, I'm an early riser.'

For an instant Mrs Gray's expression betrayed that she thought this piece of news unbelievable. 'Good, then, dear, I'm rather rushed in the mornings. The busiest part of the day.'

After she had gone Nicole moved back across the room to the bedside table. She picked up the squat glass tumbler and sniffed cautiously at the contents. Whisky, brandy? She didn't know which. She put the glass down again and sank on to the bed. For a mercy it was soft and the cotton sheets smelled of sunshine. She was very tired, badly in need of sleep. For more than six months now she hadn't been well—afraid, remorseful, haunted; as her father said, almost at breaking point. What had happened to Peter had left her emotionally crippled.

Once she had been known as the girl who had every-thing; beauty, wealth, a fine respected man for a father. Her father had never fallen victim to Peter's practised charm, but finally he had been forced into giving them his blessing. Their engagement party had been one of the big social events of the year. Nicole touched a hand to her cheek and the tears stood in her eyes. It was bad to be alone on a night like this.

She stood up and picked up her hairbrush, drawing it

through the thick, massy swing of her hair. Once this same ritual had relaxed her. Peter had always loved her hair, swearing he saw purple lights in its sheen. She had been deliriously happy then, a sheltered young girl in love for the first time in her life. In those early days she had been incapable of seeing Peter as he really was. Then later, when she had been so ill, her aunt had called him a clever and attractive opportunist, then burst into tears herself. The tragedy of Peter had hurt them all.

It didn't seem possible, even now, that she could have been in love one week, then out of it the next, but that was what happened to her, and it had precipitated Peter's death. She could never forget it, or outlive her nightmare of remorse. Less than a month after she had broken off their engagement, Peter had been killed in his speeding car and at the funeral his mother, in a paroxysm of grief, had accused Nicole of sending Peter to his death—a callous temptress who had ensnared her son, then threw him over. Peter's father had been kinder, quick to press his apologies for what his wife had cried out in her bitter pain. It had been no more than a tragic accident, one of many that happened on the roads every day.

Mrs Vaughn didn't think so, and afterwards she subjected Nicole to a cruel campaign of letters and phone calls and ghastly whispered lies, until Nicole's father had found out and had put a stop to it. Richard Lindfield was a powerful man in the city and no one was going to be allowed to make life a living hell for his positively suffering daughter. Nicole's throat constricted in memory and beads of perspiration broke out at her temples.

Why hadn't she shared her father's doubts from the beginning? Why hadn't she been swayed by his wisdom and experience? There had been nothing real and sincere in Peter, only his passion for her. And it had been a passion, a burning fever that had turned him frighteningly vindictive. He had called her all sorts of names, through which she had maintained an appalled silence, only wishing the ground would open up and swallow her. She had deplored hurting him, but in the months of their engagement he had come to lose her love and respect. It had seemed infinitely preferable then to break off an engagement rather than make a disastrous marriage.

Peter's death had come as a dreadful shock to her and the emotional battering she had been subjected to had turned her into a shadow of her former self. Once she had been impulsive and ardent, now she was a girl with a deep reserve and a heart packed in ice. It was almost like being turned into a different person. Her father, poor man, had told her over and over that she was being appallingly hard on herself, but she could only remember Peter's stricken face. It would haunt her to her dying day. Peter was weak and calculating, but he hadn't deserved to die. If she hadn't been such a poor judge of character he would never have become so deeply involved with her. Peter had told her once that she had a rare power to stir a man, but that was a quality scarcely to be desired. It had left her life in turmoil and driven Peter to a reckless self-destruction. Mrs Vaughn had indeed made her feel a criminal. Her breakdown was almost complete.

It was her father, loving his motherless daughter so deeply, who had suggested she accept Christine's warm and compassionate invitation to recuperate on Sapphire, the home station of the legendary Rossiter chain. Christine had been a good friend through their gay, sparkling, university days, and Christine had flown all the way from South-West Queensland to attend Nicole's ill-fated engagement party. Christine, never very good at hiding her feelings, had not been won over by the smooth, ambitious, Peter, but naturally refrained from saying anything that would have hurt her friend. Even through the rosy clouds that had surrounded her in those days, Nicole had been vaguely aware that quite a few of her friends were anxious about her choice of fiancé. Christine had been one of them, though she had made a valiant pretence of liking Peter at the party.

Nicole remembered now. She had cried over Christine's letter; it had touched her deeply. Helen Rossiter, Christine's mother, had included a little welcoming note that had given Nicole the strength to start on her long journey to Sapphire. In the old days she and Christine had had so much in common? How would Christine find her now? Would she still like her? In making the effort to be good company, her father and aunt had assured her that the trip would be good therapy. She hoped so, oh, how she hoped so!

Before turning off the light, she wondered briefly what kind of a man Quinn Rossiter was. If he was at all like his mother and sister, she could only meet with warm friendliness and a deep understanding. She wanted him to approve of her because after all, it was his home; Sapphire belonged to him. She had a feeling Christine had told her something else about Quinn, but she couldn't remember. There was another brother as well, Kim, and a married sister, Valerie, who had exchanged her life on an Outback cattle station for a sheep station in the South Island of New Zealand. The Rossiters were a big family clan and uncles and cousins ran the other stations in the chain. Nicole had no experience of the Outback whatever, but in her desperation it offered a wild haven.

When sleep didn't come easily, and she began to dread the thought of her night terrors, she lifted the mosquito net a fraction and sought for Mrs Gray's nightcap. Her fingers closed around the glass and she drew it back slowly towards her, thinking that she needed it. She sat up in the bed, not liking the spirit's fumes or later its fiery taste, but as Mrs Gray had promised, it relaxed her. Her last conscious thought was, she would have to be dressed and waiting for Quinn Rossiter in the morning.

CHAPTER TWO

FOR the first time in a long time, Nicole slept deeply—so deeply that the first knock on her door invoked no response. Through the healing haze of sleep she heard the second knock and she sat up in alarm, not stretching languorously nor staring bleakly as she had so often done, but springing up instantly like a startled doe.

The third knock sounded distinctly imperious, but she had her robe on, smoothing her tumbled hair and moving towards the door. After all, Mrs Gray had to wake her and probably bring a tray to her room. Her intensely dark eyes were huge and a little dazed and her magnolia face wore its look of soft melancholy.

'Mrs Gray, I'm sorry!' She opened the door swiftly, beginning to apologise, only to recoil in shock.

A man stood on the threshold, so tall and commanding, so obviously controlling his impatience, his high-mettled temper invaded the air. 'Miss Lindfield?'

His eyes were a burning blue radiance in a striking, darkly tanned face.

'Yes.' Colour stained her cheeks and her hand caught at a chiffon fold of her robe drawing it across her breast.

'Quinn Rossiter.'

He said it as though that explained everything, as indeed it did. Nicole was bewildered by his appearance and manner. He wasn't in the least like Christine—he could hardly have been more unlike her. 'Forgive me!' She was trembling and she knew he was aware of it. 'I'm afraid I slept in.'

'That all right,' he said smoothly, but there was still a reprimand in his eyes.

'It will only take me a moment to dress.'

'Take your time!' His glance skimmed her face and her slender body. He seemed quite unperturbed by her beauty of her *déshabillé*. 'I'll order you some breakfast and as soon as you're ready, we'll get away.'

She held her small head very high, but he could see the pulse throbbing away in her temple. 'It was the trip yesterday—the heat. I felt ready to collapse.'

'There's no need to apologise.'

Something in his expression made her flush violently. 'Have I made you angry?' she asked.

'However could you do that?'

She looked away quickly, striving for calmness. It was absolutely vital to remain calm, yet she had the instant urge to hit him. It was only afterwards that she felt startled by the violence of her own reaction, she who had withdrawn to her ivory tower.

'You're all right, aren't you?'

There was no trace of concern in his clipped tone and she swung back and stared into his blue, burning eyes. 'Don't worry, Mr Rossiter, I'm stronger than I look.'

He shook his head slightly and his expression didn't change. 'I'm afraid that doesn't impress me.'

She swayed slightly and his hand shot out and closed over her delicate shoulder. 'Chris didn't tell me you've been ill.'

The warmth of his hand was searing her skin. 'You've made a mistake. I'm not ill.'

'Then what's wrong with you?'

'Nothing!' She tried to keep the emotion out of her voice. 'I wasn't properly awake.'

'Do you think it fair to lie?'

'Please, Mr Rossiter!' She tried unsuccessfully to slip away from him.

'Make it Quinn. It seems only sensible if you're coming out to Sapphire.' Abruptly he released her and half turned his wide shoulders. 'What shall I order for you?'

'Just coffee would do.'

'I thought so. Be smart for once and forget your dancer's figure.'

He was gone, and his sharp ridicule lent her the impetus she needed. Within fifteen minutes she was dressed and walking into the downstairs dining room. It was quite empty, as she expected it to be at past nine in the morning. Her little passion now seemed absurd. She sat down at one of the tables and as she did so Quinn Rossiter entered the room. 'Where's your luggage?'

'Upstairs in the hallway.' She half stood up again, feeling foolish.

'I'll get it.' His dazzling blue eyes weren't warmed by her appearance. He barely seemed to glance at her.

Nicole sat very quietly and in another minute Mrs Gray wheeled a trolley through the swinging door that led to the kitchen.

'Now then, dear, how are we this morning?'

'Much better thank you, Mrs Gray, though my nightcap made me sleep in.'

'Yes, it does that sometimes,' Mrs Gray said with smiling tolerance. 'I must say you look a picture, a real city girl with your lovely face and your lovely clothes.'

Indulgently she piled dishes on the table and Nicole could see she had to eat cereal and bacon and eggs. There were two pieces of toast as well, curls of butter, honey and marmalade and a tall, silvered pot of coffee. 'This looks very nice!' Nicole ventured without looking up.

'Mr Rossiter thinks you need a little more nourishment than a bird.'

'I see.' Nicole fixed her eyes intently on the cups and saucers. There were two of each. 'Call if you need more toast,' Mrs Gray laughed with apparent enjoyment, then walked to the adjoining door. 'You haven't known Mr Rossiter very long. Don't fall in love with him like all the rest of the girls.'

'I won't, Mrs Gray,' Nicole protested, shaken out of her gentle torpor. 'I'm not at all romantic!'

'That's not important, dear. With your face romance will find you!'

The lighthearted compliment made Nicole's heart beat with pain. She dreaded the thought of ever being sought after and admired again, but at least Quinn Rossiter wasn't thrown off balance by any aspect of her appearance. In his scale of values she obviously didn't rate very high.

Valiantly she finished off the cereal, but she despaired of eating the bacon and eggs. She hardly liked to offend Mrs Gray, and Quinn Rossiter was a man of strong opinions who might force her to eat it like a child. It might be one way to please him, so she picked up a fork, but couldn't begin.

When he spoke behind her, she started almost guiltily, lifting her head and fixing her dark eyes on this naturally arrogant man who was, unbelievably, Christine's brother.

'What are you fretting about?' He pulled out a chair and sat down in it.

'I was despairing of eating so much breakfast,' she explained. 'You couldn't help me out, could you?'

He gave her a long, penetrating look that backed up his hard, no-nonsense manner. 'Surely it isn't making you cry?'

'Hardly!' she gave a little rueful shrug. 'I have to admit, though, I find a large breakfast daunting.'

'Press on, all the same!' he exhorted. 'I don't want you to faint on me.'

'Why on earth should I?'

'Why not? I can't remember when I've seen a more

fragile lady.' He poured two cups of coffee and placed one firmly by her hand. 'Drink it.'

'Thank you.' She spoke with a polite lack of expression, but he could see the sudden flash of her eyes.

'Purposely or not, Chris gave me a completely different picture of her friend Nicole,' he told her.

'Obviously you're disappointed,' she commented before she could stop herself.

He laughed beneath his breath and tipped back in the chair. 'My God, what does it matter to me anyway? A society beauty or a despairing madonna?'

'Perhaps I'm not too happy about you either!' she answered with a surprising burst of spirit.

This appeared to amuse him because he put back his head and laughed. 'So you do have a little spirit after all?'

'It's the only brave thing I've said in months!' There was something acutely disturbing about him, his hard strength and surety, the implacable *maleness*. 'How far is it to Sapphire?' she asked, and changed the subject abruptly.

'Why? Are you considering *not* coming?'

'All right!' She looked back at him, recognising the hard calculation in his face. 'I surrender and I'll come quietly. You're not in the least like Chris, are you?'

'My dear, does this mean you don't like me?' Their eyes met and Nicole found she couldn't look away. She would never be able to handle a man like Quinn Rossiter and she was sure she didn't want to try.

'I'm doing my best to like you,' she said in a quickened tone, 'but it's not strictly essential, is it?'

'No.' He stretched out his hand and caught her wrist. 'Eat the rest of that toast.'

'I'm sorry, I *can't*!' The hard strength of his hand seemed to make her frantic.

'For me!' His blue eyes mocked her. 'I've decided to

be kind to you, Nicole. Perhaps I've misjudged you.'

In her anxiety she did as she was told, finishing off the piece of toast and draining her coffee cup. 'I could see the impatience in your eyes,' she said, and her voice was low and pleading. 'I know you don't believe me, but that's the first sleep-in I've had in a long time.'

'But I do believe you,' he answered briefly. 'You're not happy, are you? Speak up, little one, I'm not as cruel and uncaring as you think.'

For an instant tears blinded her and she struggled up from the table, weakened and confused by his effect on her. No doubt he would think her very strange, at the least neurotic.

'Stop that!'

He held her and she stood there, trembling and chilled despite the morning's heat. She heard herself saying confusedly, 'I haven't been well, you must remember.'

'What are you running away from?' he asked urgently. 'A love affair, some man?' His expression was alert and fixed, blue eyes blazing down at her.

'Didn't Christine tell you anything about me?' She pressed her fingers against her temples and he shook her slightly.

'What is there to tell? You've got calamity written all over you. You're trembling all over and you're nearly hysterical.' He took his hand away, regarding her gravely. 'Sensibly, Chris didn't alarm me. She merely asked permission to invite a very dear friend from her university days.'

'Oh!' Nicole replied faintly, and didn't lift her head.

'So what are you frightened of?'

'Nothing!' Her dark eyes flashed almost scornfully and her cheeks flushed a dusky pink.

'I hope you're right!' As though alerted to the least sound or movement he stopped speaking just as Mrs Gray came through the connecting door.

'Enjoy your breakfast?' she asked Nicole brightly.

'You'll have to forgive her, Mrs Gray,' Quinn Rossiter said calmly. 'She's hardly touched anything.'

Mrs Gray inspected the table but spared Nicole a lecture. 'Don't worry, dear, your appetite will pick up as soon as you settle in to your holiday.'

'Thank you, Mrs Gray!' Nicole smiled at the older woman, who seemed to be regarding her compassionately.

Hands clenched, she followed Quinn Rossiter out of the dining room and into the wide hallway with Mrs Gray bringing up the respectful rear of the procession.

'Got all your things now, have you, dear?' she glanced down at Nicole's expensive luggage over the top of her spectacles. 'You don't want to forget anything.'

'It's all right, I've checked,' Quinn Rossiter returned carelessly. 'Come along now, Nicole, you look as if you need to sit down again.'

His hard, mocking attitude towards her was inexplicable. She felt stunned, quite unable to see him in the light of Christine's brother. Not only was he as dark as Christine was fair, but he appeared to lack the two factors that had always drawn Nicole to Christine; generosity and kindness. She was quite sure in her heart that if he knew the truth about her he would never show her pity. It would be difficult to hide anything from those brilliant blue eyes, and the challenge of his manner had her quivering emotionally.

Mrs Gray continued to fuss over her all the way out to the rather battered station wagon that was parked in the scant shade of a tree that grew a few yards from the front entrance of the hotel. There Quinn Rossiter broke in on her polite little goodbyes as if the gentle sweetness of her voice was yet another one of her peculiarities, then she was sitting beside him in the vehicle while Mrs Gray stood waving them off.

'Cheer up, you'll be back!' he said dryly.

She turned her face to him, halted by his tone. Something about him was making her ache inside and it was all she could do not to burst into tears. 'Mrs Gray was very kind to me,' she said defensively.

'Naturally!' His gaze slipped over her quickly as though he caught the faint hysteria within her. 'It all sounds pretty silly, but you'd fit a lot of her romantic notions. Beautiful, expensive, a classic face full of untold secrets, the most extravagant nightwear she's ever likely to see in her life.'

Their eyes met briefly, and she hated the amusement and mockery in his eyes. 'Go on,' she said. 'At this point I'm quite sure you're making fun of me.'

'On the contrary, Nicole, I'm trying to jolly you along. I realise now you're on the verge of some kind of breakdown.'

'I am not!' She shook back her dark hair almost violently.

'You're brooding about it right now. For God's sake, what *is* it? I find it odd Chris didn't fill me in a little.'

'Perhaps she didn't want to antagonise you.' The hard edge in his voice forced her nervous, brittle laugh.

'Very neat, and you're right. I'm just as surprised as I could be. You're quite different from all her other friends.'

'And what does that mean?' Her hand tightened on the seat and she turned her head away, breathing deeply.

His brief laugh was rough-edged. 'Most of them come out to enjoy themselves, or find a little excitement. You're on the run from someone or something. I might have been told earlier.'

'Perhaps you'd like to leave me here!' she said huskily, and the tears started to her eyes.

'Quite possibly,' he returned very shortly. 'What is it that's hurt you so badly?'

'Why is it that you want to know?' Despite herself she had to turn to him and her dark eyes were pleading and liquid.

'It occurs to me if I do, I might be able to avert trouble. Or at least, I hope so.' The hard, beautiful mouth went wry with irony.

'I told you,' her head drooped again, 'I haven't been well for a long time, but I'm quite all right now. Christine and I always got on well together. She often asked me out to Sapphire in the old days, so I've decided to come.'

'Have it your own way!' His dark brows came together and he put his foot down harder on the accelerator so that the station wagon leapt forward down the rough scrub track that was obviously a short cut to the airfield. 'By the way,' his voice rose slightly above the noise of the screeching cockatoos that flew up into the air like huge white flowers, 'you're overdressed for the climate.'

'I'm sorry!' Nicole knew that now without a doubt. Her outfit might have been perfect anywhere else. If so, it wasn't here. Her tomato red soft linen blazer was meant to go over the olive green silk shirt and colour-matched linen skirt and her high-heeled leather sandals matched the soft red of her jacket, but obviously it hadn't been a good choice for a morning of soaring heat.

He glanced at her again with cool deliberation. 'If you get the jacket off you might be more comfortable. It's very chic, I'll admit, but all for nothing. Can't you see the heat shimmering past the windows?'

'Yes, I can,' she replied gently, and her lovely face went remote. 'I just thought it would all be rather different.'

'You mean you thought *I* was going to be quite different?' he challenged her with a turbulent flash in his blue, burning eyes. Antagonism seemed to be flowing from him and Nicole found herself actually shuddering.

'Well, yes,' she confessed. 'I was prepared to meet ... hoping to meet ... someone like Christine.'

'But it's quite simple, Nicole,' he drawled sardonically, 'and obviously you're just finding out. Chris is my half-sister. My father remarried when I was a boy. My own mother just couldn't take the savage land. A case of another marriage not going according to plan. She was something like you in type; ravishingly inadequate. At any rate she left us, my father and me.'

'And you've never forgiven her?'

'I don't think about it any more!' he returned bluntly. 'You're not afraid of light aircraft, are you?'

'Only human relationships, Mr Rossiter,' she murmured, and her low, gentle voice went quite brittle.

'Well, I knew that as soon as I laid eyes on you,' he observed coolly. 'The trouble is your kind of looks invite drama.' His brilliant gaze leapt over her creamy, magnolia face. 'A madonna, except for your eyes and your mouth. I've always found those particular features are the best guide to a woman's true nature.'

'I couldn't argue with you, Mr Rossiter,' she answered without emotion, though a dull anger or excitement was making her heart beat erratically.

He turned his head away and his dark sardonic face held a cruel amusement. 'We're almost there. You *are* coming with me, aren't you, little one?'

'Yes, of course.'

'I can't say you sound too happy about it.'

'I'm sure I'll get used to you, Mr Rossiter!' she returned instantaneously.

'I'm not looking for understanding.' His dark head was tilted back a little, his blue eyes narrowed against the blinding glare of the sun. 'If you're going to survive at all, you'll have to learn to relax.'

'I try to!' She shook her head a little sadly.

'Meanwhile the situation worsens. You haven't a husband somewhere you're running away from?'

'No, *no*!'

'Why so intense? You're nearly wringing your hands. Anyway, I knew the answer to that one. What about love affairs?'

'Plenty!' she answered bitterly.

'Well, someone has taught you to suffer!' he returned bluntly and with no shade of compassion. 'I'm fascinated by your manner. You're afraid of men.'

'Yes, very!' she returned with a flash of rebellion, even indignation. 'Don't have too much contempt for me, please!'

'Are you sure that's what it is?' He glanced at her side-long and there were little sparks of mockery in his dazzling blue eyes. 'Tell me about your childhood,' he demanded as though she had never shown that betraying flash of anger.

'It was very happy.'

'So your psyche has been damaged since?'

Her lips formed words, but she found she couldn't speak. Let him see she was defeated. He had already worked that out for himself. Through the thinning trees she could see the airstrip and she gave an audible sigh of relief. Quinn Rossiter made her feel threatened and something else she couldn't yet identify.

They bumped across the open ground until they ran up on to the tarmac and Nicole looked about her. The light aircraft that stood on the strip was much bigger than she expected, twin-engined and impressive, the luxury automobile of the Outback. Inside the cabin they would be even more enclosed than they were now.

'Try not to look as though you're being kidnapped!' Quinn Rossiter said to her transparent face.

'I can't seem to please you whatever my expression.'

'It happens!' he drawled laconically, and brought the vehicle to a halt outside the small office building that stood on the site.

Nicole must have given a little gasp of dismay, for he

turned to smile at her sharply. Against his darkly tanned skin, his teeth were very white and she realised a lot of women would find him both dangerous and exciting. But there was a hardness about him, a dominance that made her shrink into herself; a sensuality, a vibrant male sexuality that she wanted to shut out like the blinding brilliance of the sun.

He made a jeering little noise in his throat, then swung out of the car just as a tall, middle-aged man emerged from the office.

'Hi there, Quinn!'

'Harry!' He walked towards the other man with the kind of lithe grace Nicole was becoming used to, taking the man's hand and saying something that had the other man laughing. Nicole's face burned, then paled. Perhaps he was saying something about her. She fumbled with the seat belt, but he was back beside her to hold the door.

'Here, let me help you.'

'It's quite all right, really!'

'Have it your own way. I've never met a girl so super-defensive!'

The man called Harry moved over to join them and Quinn introduced them while Harry studied Nicole openly and with immense approval. 'Sure is easy to see you're a city lady!'

'Sure is!' Quinn seconded dryly, contemplating Nicole's magnolia face with brilliant scorn. 'Go and sit in the shade, little one, while I have a few words with Harry.'

'I'd rather look at the plane. What is it?'

'Beech Baron,' Harry returned warmly. 'You can relax, miss, Quinn here is a skilled pilot with plenty of experience.'

'I'm sure!' she said in her soft, sweet voice, though she felt a little faint and wobbly. She longed for privacy and a cool room, but she was committed now to go along with

Quinn Rossiter, a man who noticed her slightest little discomfiture and used it against her. If only Christine had come with him! The vast, flat sea of plain swam before her eyes. The land looked hostile, dramatically so, a burning, limitless wilderness that made her afraid.

She smiled at Harry and wandered away, fixing her eyes on the aircraft that would take them to Sapphire. She had never flown in anything smaller than a medium-sized jet and she pushed her hand across her eyes. There was no breeze to move the dark mass of her hair, no cloud in the densely blue sky. Anxiety pressed about her like a living thing. It was bad enough saying goodbye to her father and Aunt Sara, now her disturbing encounter with Christine's brother was convincing her she was making another mistake. She had come all these miles to escape, but she knew that she carried her past with her. Quinn Rossiter had already read tension and suffering in her face.

When strong hands touched her shoulders she swung around in near-fright, seeing the intense, watchful expression come back into his eyes. 'You're much, much too highly strung and you can't keep it up. Here, give me your jacket.'

'I wouldn't dream of arguing with you, Mr Rossiter!'

A taut silence fell while he drew the soft linen blazer from her narrow shoulders. 'That should feel better, surely?'

'Yes, it does.' She couldn't meet that brilliant blue scrutiny, so she lowered her eyes.

Harry's footsteps echoed on the tarmac as he walked across to them and loaded her two suitcases into the cabin. 'Hope to see you again, Miss Lindfield,' he said pleasantly. 'Excuse me now, that's the phone. Anything else I can do for you, Quinn?'

'No, thanks a lot, Harry.'

'Regards to the family. Enjoy yourself now, Miss Lindfield. I guess you know you're a very lucky girl. Sapphire's our greatest asset in this part of the world!' He gave them both a quick little salute and hurried back to the office where the telephone was ringing insistently.

'Come along, Nicole,' Quinn Rossiter said smoothly though his dark face seemed to harden, 'it's clear you're in need of a long holiday.' He put his hand to her elbow and she felt herself being inexorably compelled towards the cabin door.

Five minutes later she was strapped into the co-pilot's seat, pushing back as the aircraft commenced its forward surge into flight. The wind was rushing around the wing, building up the lift, then the nose lifted and they were climbing at full power into the peacock blue heavens.

Nicole's racing heart began to quieten and she looked down and out over the brooding ochre plains. Seen from the air the vast landscape had a harsh kind of magnificence and she sank back gratefully into her seat, conscious of the cooler air.

'You look pale. Are you all right?'

'I have a naturally white skin.'

'I've noticed that!' He met her dark eyes. 'If you want to keep it perfect you'd better wear a decent wide-brimmed hat at all times.'

'I do have one!' she said as though he was putting her on her mettle.

'Good girl!' he answered a little tersely. 'It might have been more pleasant for you had you come in the cooler months, but then, I suppose, there was no special reason.'

She accepted the taunt silently. It was going to be very awkward for her if she angered him, yet it seemed her whole aura had set up some kind of conflict that could be harmful.

'What do you do, Nicole?' he asked suavely.

'Do?'

'For a living,' he said dryly.

She saw his picture of her in her mind's eye, but she couldn't change it. 'I act as a hostess to my father. I try to help him as much as I can. We do a lot of entertaining.'

'It all sounds very arduous!' he mocked her.

'Not really, but at different times I've been kept very busy.'

'Your mother is dead, then?'

She turned her dark head towards him, her almond eyes grave. 'She died before I had the chance to know her.'

'And you're an only child?'

'I would have preferred brothers and sisters.'

'It hurts, does it?'

'Some days everything hurts!' she said sombrely, unable to conceal the pain in her voice.

'You bruise too easily,' he said as though he had thought about it.

'I suppose so.' Her eyes shifted from the instrument panels to his hand on the controls. It was lean and brown and beautifully shaped. A strong, responsible hand, ruthless perhaps. She couldn't allow herself to become intimidated. Hands like that could certainly bruise. . . .

To her relief he began to talk about the territory they were passing over, pointing out landmarks, the line of eroded hills, the flat and featureless plains, the silver billabongs that were strung out along the dried-up river. At intervals she asked questions, just wanting to please him until gradually she noticed the character of the countryside change.

'We're almost there,' he said quietly, yet something in his voice gave deeper meaning to his words. Pride and possession vibrated there and found some answering chord in Nicole.

'You love it, don't you?'

'There's nowhere else I want to be.'

'Yet it must be lonely?'

'It depends on one's nature. Sapphire is my life. It has a history and a future. I'm just the keeper of the flame.'

'Then you must want a son and heir?'

'You can see that I might!' His voice was cool to the point of curtness. She could see that she had aroused a reaction and perversely it pleased her. There had been a palpable antagonism between them, right from the beginning.

'There's also the matter of a wife,' she said sweetly and lightly. 'Have you anyone in mind?'

'Wait and see!' He glanced at her fleetingly and his blue eyes seemed frankly malicious.

'I haven't annoyed you, have I?'

His mouth shaped itself into magnificent scorn. 'How, Nicole? You've obviously grown accustomed to having men grovelling at your feet.'

'Not in the least!' she said shortly. 'It's the last thing I want.'

'You must know you can't avoid it. All you need to tell me now is that you're on the run from some particularly violent lover.'

She whitened visibly and the whiteness remained.

'All right, Nicole,' something cold crept into his voice, 'if it will make you relax I promise you'll be safe on Sapphire. No one is going to waylay you or force you into marriage.'

'*Please* . . .' her voice sank to a husky softness, 'wouldn't it be better if we don't discuss me at all?'

'Perhaps!' He sounded amused. 'You're the kind of woman it would be wise to keep at a safe distance.' His blue eyes flicked her tender, creamy face. 'However, I suppose we'd better start again. You might try calling me Quinn. It should come easily with practice.'

'I'll remember.'

'But you can't manage it now.' His eyes mocked her.

'I don't know you yet.'

'I see. Chris will introduce us.'

Nicole flushed and subsided into silence. Beneath them and as far as the eyes could see was Sapphire, thousands of square miles of secret, rugged country, of purple ranges and red sandhills and an elaborate network of water-bearing streams. She felt very small in the great emptiness. Her whole life had been lived in a big city where space was at a premium, it seemed difficult now to contemplate such sheer immensity. It would have taken greatness to carve a giant holding out of such primeval land with all its dangers and privations; greatness to hold it. She remembered now what Mrs Gray had called Quinn Rossiter—the strong one. He looked it. But he was a difficult man, a complex man, so forceful she doubted if she could ever feel anything else but unease in his presence. More, pure fear, and she couldn't explain it.

As they flew deeper into this feudal station fascinated she could see giant letters spelling SAPPHIRE and the markers that lined the all-weather runway. Buildings appeared out of the trees, white buildings that argued careful planning and not haphazard design. It was like seeing a small township from the air and she was conscious of a feeling of being overwhelmed. This was a different world from the one she had moved in all her life. How could she fit in there? There was anxiety in her mind and the contraction of her stomach muscles.

They were losing altitude fast, homing in like a white bird to the runway. The flaps were down and they were coming into the final glide. Nicole found herself breath-

ing unevenly, but Quinn Rossiter was cool and unconcerned.

'Welcome to Sapphire, little one!' he said at the precise
moment they touched down.

Christine was there to greet them, her face shining with
pleasure and excitement, her arms outstretched to em-
brace her friend. 'Nicky darling, how lovely to have you
here. I can scarcely believe it!'

Everything about her, the remembered warmth and
sincerity of her manner, brought the quick, emotional
tears to Nicole's intensely dark eyes. 'Oh, Chris!' she
whispered, but couldn't get any further.

'Isn't she beautiful?' Christine was asking happily.
'What did I tell you?'

'Not enough, I think!' Quinn observed rather force-
fully.

'Don't be disagreeable!' Christine threw up her fair
head to smile at him. 'Thanks a lot, Big Brother. Was it a
good trip?'

'Smooth as ice.' He slanted a glance over Nicole's
lovely, tearful face. 'Why don't you take Nicole up to the
house? It's plain you two girls have a lot to catch up on.'

'You bet!' Christine was bubbling over with excitement. 'Mother is so looking forward to meeting you,
Nick. She's heard so much about you.'

'Unlike *me*!' Quinn rejoined suavely.

The heat was shimmering all around them and Quinn
turned his head over his shoulder and gestured to a young
aboriginal attendant who was hovering uncertainly.

'Stow the luggage in the Land Rover, Paddy.'

'Sure, Boss!' Dazzling white teeth appeared in a smile.

'The cartons and packages are to be delivered to the
boys.'

Paddy grinned some more. 'Bring me records, Boss?'

'I did. Tracked them down when I really didn't have the time.'

'Thanks, Boss!' Paddy slammed the door and saluted, his stiffened hand coming smartly to his slouch hat. 'Anythin' else?'

'Come over here. This is Paddy,' Quinn said when the youth reached them. 'The best jackeroo on the station. Best tracker after his grandfather.'

Paddy's big black eyes looked proud but vulnerable. He waited and Nicole smiled.

'I'm happy to meet you, Paddy.'

Paddy answered the smile, then looked quickly at the ground.

'Thanks, Paddy,' Quinn said evenly. 'It will be your pleasant duty to ride along with the girls beyond the easy trails.'

'Yes, Boss. Don't want nothin' terrible to happen to them.'

'Exactly.' Quinn waved him away with a warning. 'Remember to keep the noise down. Not everyone admires rock groups.'

Christine laughed. 'Why don't you tell him to haul off to the bush? It won't be peaceful around here for a week.'

Quinn shrugged lightly. 'I believe in encouraging my best boys. There are worse hobbies.' He turned his head back nonchalantly and smiled at Nicole, his infrequent smile that so lit and softened his face and made something stir in her like a disturbing tremor. 'Come, Nicole, you've been standing around long enough!'

Christine put her arm around her friend's narrow waist, then they were all moving over to the Land Rover. 'Coming up with us?' Christine's blue eyes sought her stepbrother's face.

'I won't get involved in all your girlish chitchat, if you don't mind.'

'Don't take any notice of him, Nick!' Christine warned. 'No one could be more considerate, kind, or thoughtful.'

'Really?' Despite herself Nicole studied the arrogant dark face with open disbelief.

'Nicole isn't close to me like you are,' he returned dryly. 'She can't see any softness in me anywhere.'

Christine looked from one to the other with some interest. 'Nick will know you a whole lot better in several weeks.'

'There you are, Nicole,' he smiled at her, 'if you're looking for consolation.'

'Thank you for coming for me,' she said, and her voice was politely impersonal. 'I realise you must be a very busy man.'

'Hey now, why so formal?' Christine asked, half laughing, half serious, 'I want you two to be friends, not sparring partners.'

'Then Nicole will have to creep out of her shell, just as far as she knows how.'

The brilliant eyes were challenging, submerging her in their blueness. 'Perhaps I will!' she said a little shortly. Quinn Rossiter was an impossible man. He even made her breathe fast.

Her heart was still pumping furiously as they drove away in the Land Rover. It didn't occur to her until much later that what she was experiencing was pure feeling after months of being frozen in her misery. At least Christine was still the same, and she was looking at her anxiously.

'It's been bad for you, hasn't it?' she commented.

'It must show.'

Christine's blue eyes were warm. 'Oh, no, you're as lovely as ever.'

'Your brother saw through me in a minute.'

'You sound worried,' observed Christine.

'I just wondered what you told him.'

Christine's smile was crooked. 'I told him we were at uni together and I cared a lot about you. I told him you were beautiful and very, very sexy and you were completely unconcerned with either. I didn't tell him anything about your engagement or about Peter.'

'I think he might judge me harshly,' Nicole ventured.

'Oh, no!' Christine reached out and patted her friend's hand for emphasis. 'You don't know Quinn. I adore him. So does Mother and Val. Kim thinks the sun rises and sets on him. You'll be meeting Kim in a day or two. He's on Willunga, making a few investigations for Quinn. Kim has plenty of initiative and enthusiasm and Quinn likes to reward him. He's taking over more and more of our affairs. It takes a good deal of the burden off Quinn and leaves him free to handle more important matters. Quinn's not an easy person, I'll admit, but then what remarkable man ever is? Around here, we all gaze at him worshipfully!'

'Maybe authority leaves its mark,' Nicole said with faint amusement. 'He was very clear-eyed about me. He took one look at me and asked point blank what exactly had happened to me.'

'And you told him?'

'No.' Nicole moistened her dry lips. 'It will be a long time before I can talk about Peter. I just know in my bones your brother wouldn't understand.'

'It was Peter's wretched mother that made you feel so shockingly guilty!' Christine's blue eyes glittered with feeling. 'What right had she to punish you for an act of fate? Her behaviour was inhuman. Anyway, you're here to forget it. Mother and I are going to see to it!' she added more gently.

Neither girl spoke for a few seconds, then Nicole said

in almost a voice of wonder, as though she had woken from a half-trance, 'It's big, isn't it? Endless!'

Christine was smiling again. 'Do I detect a note of awe?'

'You do.' Nicole turned her head to look out of the big wrap-around windows. 'There were thousands of head grazing as we came in, beautiful-looking beasts. Some were resting under the trees and some were drinking at the streams. I've never seen anything like it. One doesn't realise just how big the country is.'

'Everybody knows Queensland is more than twice the size of Texas!' Christine said in an exaggerated drawl. 'The buildings you can see to the right and left of us are the staff bungalows and cookhouse. There are offices and the station store, sheds for machinery and timber and all kinds of gear. We're all but self-sufficient. We grow our own fruit and vegetables, raise chickens, keep our own dairy herd. The holding yards and the sales ring are much further away. You can see those tomorrow when you've rested. You must be tired after all your travelling.'

'Enough to sleep in this morning,' Nicole said wryly. A small movement caught her eye, a flash of colour, then another. 'Are they parrots?'

'You'll see thousands of them. Ring-necked parrots in the mulga, galahs and corellas along the watercourses and on the plains when they feed, millions of little budgies and crimson chats and wrens, the hawks and the falcons chasing the finches, the eagles soaring over the hill country, the lignum swamps and the billabongs jam-packed with water birds. It's a major breeding ground for nomadic water birds around here. I've so much to show you, so many wonderful sights. I can't think how I've ever let you delay your trip so long.'

'You've always been a good friend to me, Chris,' Nicole said quietly. 'The letter you sent me, you and your mother, made me cry.'

'Poor baby, you've had a bad time of it, but you've reached Sapphire now!'

Until they were almost upon it, the homestead lay hidden in its oasis of magnificent gums, so when it rose up before them Nicole drew in her breath in delight.

'Oh, Chris, you never told me you lived in a mansion!'

'Indisputedly that's what it is!' Christine returned with pride. 'All the more heart-stopping in the middle of nowhere.'

'It looks loved,' said Nicole, looking out at the beautiful, serene homestead, symmetrical and formal like most Georgian buildings, but glowing with the colour of rosy bricks and frosty white pillars and balconies and the shutters that were fixed to the windows of both storeys. It was a big, handsome house by anyone's standards and its classic lines were softened by the surrounding grove of greenery and the gardens that were drowning in colour and scent. Some very beautiful yellow-flowered vine clung to the downstairs balcony and spilled over its white cast-iron lace to the massed blue hydrangeas below. Colour filled Nicole's cheeks and her lovely sad face took on a new life.

'I almost feel as if I've been here before. It's not at all strange to me. I remember the fan lights and the side lights on the front door, how slender the columns are that support the veranda.'

'Perhaps you were here in another life!' Christine smiled at her tone of enchantment. 'I can see a change in you even in half an hour!' As she spoke she brought the Land Rover to a halt in the cool shade of one of the magnificent old trees, and just at that moment a woman appeared at the open front door, then smiled and waved and walked across the veranda and down into the sunlight.

'Here's Mother!' Christine said unnecessarily, for the petite, youthful-looking woman who advanced on them so smilingly was so like Christine, Nicole would have recognised her anywhere.

'Mrs Rossiter!' She was out of the car, holding out her hand.

'Nicole dear, how lovely to have you!'

'How very kind of you to ask me. I think this is the loveliest place I've ever seen.'

'Ah, yes, we love it!' Helen Rossiter studied her with her daughter's large, candid eyes. 'Are you tired, dear?'

'Not so very much now.' Nicole looked around her. 'It was a good flight. I hope I didn't take Quinn from anything important?'

'He was most insistent that he would collect you himself and he took the Baron, which means you have a V.I.P. rating. Where is he, by the way?'

'Wild horses wouldn't drag Quinn into girl-talk!' Christine told her with a laugh.

'Come in, dear!' Helen said kindly. 'We've planned a special dinner tonight to welcome you, but you'll like to relax for the rest of the day. Travelling can be very tiring, I know.'

Inside everything looked very rich and mellow. The hallway was spacious, high-ceilinged, as were all the rooms of the house. Nicole received impression after impression on her way to the bedroom that had been specially prepared for her. The house was more beautiful than she could have imagined, more opulent, more romantic. The walls shimmered lightly in contrast to the dark, antique furniture and there was softness and colour in paintings and gilt-framed mirrors, the richness of fabric and the delicacy of flowers.

'This is heaven. Absolute heaven!' Nicole said, leaning out of the open bedroom window that looked over a massed garden and a parkland of trees.

Christine looked at her mother and smiled. 'We aim to please, don't we, Mamma?'

'It's good to have you here, dear,' Helen Rossiter said with quiet sincerity. 'Christine has told me of your great hurt and unhappiness. I can see you're a very sensitive girl, but after a time if you let it you'll find great consolation in the land itself, the space and the peace and the freedom. Just remember, dear, we're your friends. If you want to talk, let it out. If you want to be silent, we'll respect that. Christine has always spoken of you with great affection and admiration too. I want you to look on us as family.'

The blue eyes that looked into Nicole's were alive with understanding and reassurance and a certain tenderness as well. On an impulse Nicole crossed the room and kissed the older woman's cheek. 'Thank you so much, Mrs Rossiter. I feel it already!'

'Aunt Helen, then. You can't keep calling me Mrs Rossiter.'

'Aunt Helen,' said Nicole. 'I'd like that.'

'Now what about a lovely cup of tea?' Helen suggested, communicating her pleasure. 'I'll go and get it ready.'

'We'll be down in a minute,' Christine agreed. She turned to her friend and smiled. 'You were wise to come to us, Nicky. I can feel it in my bones!'

CHAPTER THREE

It was shortly before midnight when Nicole became aware of the continuous pain in her left ear. She knew the cause. Flying always affected her ears to some degree and she had been experiencing the sensation of 'popping' on and off for most of the day, though it hadn't bothered her unduly. She expected it to ease and she had been so fascinated by her tour of the house and the immediate grounds the slight discomfort had paled to almost nothingness.

Aunt Helen and Christine with their warmth and their lovely, easy manners had indeed made her feel part of the family instead of an invited guest, and even Quinn had been content to indulge her over dinner, smiling to himself a little, his blue eyes studying her with a deliberation that brought colour to her cheeks and a quick end to her cool reserve. Even in one short afternoon she had come to realise that here on his empire he wielded great power, and his womenfolk regarded him with both love and reverence. For herself Nicole was sure so much power and unswerving allegiance was bad for a man, especially one who had been born with more than his share of self-confidence.

A frantic search revealed that she hadn't brought any aspirin. The pain was nagging, but not bad enough to suggest a perforated eardrum. She had been going to ask Christine for a few tablets shortly before dinner, but it had proved so delicious and she had been so unexpectedly hungry, she had forgotten. For a few seconds she stood in the centre of her lovely quiet bedroom arguing with herself. She could try to sleep and hope the pain would go away or she could take some kind of medication. The family had retired; not that she had seen Quinn, he had gone out straight after dinner, but at least she knew how to find the first aid room, as liberally stocked as a small pharmacy. The house was so big and the bedrooms so soundproofed it was unlikely she would disturb anyone if she went downstairs. She might as well get it over with, then perhaps she could be comfortable.

In the long gallery she discovered several wall brackets had been left on, and they cast shadows over the paintings and the carved mahogany chairs that were set at intervals. There were women there; pale, pretty women with folded hands, and handsome, severely elegant men. The dazzling blue eyes in the last portrait stared out relentlessly at Nicole. She knew who he was—Luke Rossiter, Quinn's grandfather. He was Christine's too, of course, and Valerie's and Kim's, but Nicole had seen other family photographs where Helen's looks and colouring were reproduced. Quinn was the only one of them to relate uncannily to the bright, fixed eyes. There was no portrait of his father, none of the mother who had so wounded her child. Child and man, Quinn Rossiter would never forgive a woman who had rejected him.

She looked over the gallery and down at the carved stairway that split into two at the first level. There was a golden pool of light at the base of the stairs, but beyond, the darkness seemed complete. She wasn't in the least afraid of the house, in fact she loved it. Her hand fell away from the gallery and she flew down the stairs as if a breeze was blowing her, her floating robe a pale shimmer in the gloom. The first aid room was to the rear of the house, past the study and the gunroom. Her hand brushed a silent, bronze statue. There was a sconce somewhere just near it.

The house was so quiet the sound of an unhurried footstep behind her had her spinning and on the defensive, aware who it was even before he spoke.

'I see it's true what they say, witches do walk after midnight!'

'I'm sorry, you ... startled me!' She couldn't smile at him and she even shrank a little when his hand went out past her shoulder to flick on the light.

'Suppose you tell me what you're wandering around for?'

'I have an earache,' she countered in a low tone, and touched the white skin of her temple. 'I was going to take a few aspirin and hope that they worked.' She was very aware of being alone with him. Very aware of what she looked like, the shadow blue of the thin chiffon, her own body beneath. She was afraid of this man, afraid of too many things. It was impossible! There was intensity in her dark eyes as she spun on her heel and moved swiftly away from him. After all, she had told him exactly what she intended doing.

She struck her knee against a heavy armchair that melted into the gloom and couldn't suppress a cry of pain.

'Oh!'

'There you are, you deserved it, rushing away like that!' He turned her by the shoulder, his fingers tightening. 'Try to see me as an ordinary human, not some devil in disguise. It's this way. Better stay with me, then you'll be spared those little whimpers.'

'I feel better now,' she told him.

'I wouldn't doubt it. If I let you go you'd run away upstairs and cry yourself to sleep. Come on, little one—after all, you did come down for aspirin!'

She had to let him lead her into the first aid room that sprang to dazzling brightness at the flick of a switch. She knew there were evening gowns far more revealing than her nightgown and the matching robe, yet she wished desperately that she had a trench coat to bury herself in.

Quinn was silent, his dark face amused, taller than ever when she was only wearing satin slippers. His dark curling hair was crisp and wind-tousled, his blue denim bush shirt unbuttoned almost to the waist to reveal a hard, muscled chest with a fine matting of dark hair and the ridge of a scar near his collarbone.

Damn him! Nicole clenched her teeth and turned away, opening out one of the wall cabinets just above her head. It was well stocked with every bottle and jar labelled by number, yet she couldn't see aspirin.

'You won't find them there,' he said smoothly, from over her shoulder. 'Better let me help you out before your nerve breaks.'

'I can't think what you're talking about!' She turned around to him, her eyes shining, her hair swinging dark and seductive against her white skin.

'Oh yes, you can!' he countered rather sternly. 'Now I'll tell you where the aspirin are kept and I'm sure you'll remember the next time.'

'Thank you.'

'It's a privilege for me to be able to put you out of pain. I even have some drops that might help you.'

'What is this going to cost?' she asked with an attempt at humour.

'Oh, maybe a smile!' he stated abruptly, and opened up a small cabinet on the far wall. 'All the minor remedies here. Does it make sense?'

'Yes, Doctor!'

'You must admit my appearance was well timed. How else would you have found them? Plus the rest of the therapy. If you'll let me I'll put one or two drops in your ear. Which one is it?'

'It's all right, I prefer to do it myself.'

'Never mind, I've a good bedside manner.'

He moved towards her and her heart leapt in her breast so violently she cried in near fear. 'I don't want you to touch me!'

'Steady!' His voice cracked out crisp and authoritative, his eyes so coldly brilliant Nicole found herself apologising in the very next breath.

'Please, I'm sorry. I don't know what made me say that.' Her dark eyes, huge and intense, were pleading with him for some kind of forgiveness.

'You're a strange girl,' he said broodingly, a certain harshness in his tone. 'Who has handled you so brutally?'

'No one. Nothing!' She put a hand to her loose hair and pushed it behind her small, aching ear. 'If you'd be kind enough?'

'Yes, ma'am. You'll come out of this easy, I promise you!'

She bit her lip and waited, in an agony because she had made a magnificent job of antagonising him.

'Have you had this kind of thing before?' he asked distantly.

'Oh yes, but it always goes away by the next day.'

'Be honest with me. Is it very painful?'

'No, not really. Just a simple earache, I think.'

'Probably, you'd be damned well screaming if you'd perforated your eardrum.'

With his fingers he gently explored all around her ear, while she stood quietly in front of him. 'Glad you came, Nicole?'

'Oh, yes!' Her eyes brushed the scar near his collar-bone. 'I could love Aunt Helen like the mother I've never known.' There was a current flowing from his fingers, a slow burning. 'Chris and I have always understood one another. And the house is so beautiful—I never guessed!'

'We've done our best to make it habitable,' he returned

blandly. 'By the way, Kim will be back the day after to-morrow. He'll certainly be glad to meet you, but I should warn you a voice has been raised to claim him. Her name's Rosalind—a lovely girl, pretty and practical and well known to us.'

The implication was clear and she could feel heat reach her nerve ends. 'I pity the woman who gets you!' she snapped.

'Oh, well, some love to suffer!' He gave her a mocking, downward glance. 'Stay still now, I'll put the drops in.'

'Thank you. I'm taking the easy way out. Like Paddy, I don't want anything terrible to happen to me.'

'But things *will* happen. Won't they, Nicole?'

She had to control herself. She had to tilt her head to the side and suffer the touch of his hand on her skin. Afterwards he made her hold her head still for a minute, then when she straightened it, he was holding out two white tablets on the palm of his hand.

'I think you're wonderfully brave!'

Swiftly she swallowed the tablets with water.

'I know what you think of me!' she answered rather shortly, and the colour in her cheeks accentuated the velvety darkness of her eyes.

'You don't know!' He smiled condescendingly. 'Emotionally, you're retarded, which is just as well because you're as beautiful as a goddess.'

'Don't suppose goddesses enjoy themselves!' she retorted, and there was more than a trace of bitter exhaustion in her tone.

'They make others suffer as well!' His blue eyes glittered with quick accusation. 'Don't deny it, Nicole!'

'I doubt very much if I could.'

They stood facing each other and Nicole shook her dark head despairingly. 'Why do you feel I owe you my life story?'

'Maybe you ought to write a book,' he told her. 'I

vaguely remember now Chris's flying out to attend some girl friend's engagement party, about seven or eight months ago. I can't be sure, but I can easily track down the date.'

'What an unpleasant thing to do!' She was trembling now and about to whirl away from him.

'Was it you?' he asked curtly.

'Oh, yes!' Her lips parted in silent pain. 'I might as well tell you, you're determined to find out. The engagement didn't work. It was broken off.'

'So why all the despair? Do you still love him?'

For an instant she didn't move, then she threw up her hand with a terrible yearning to hurt him as he was hurting her. He caught her hand in mid-air and she gasped with pain, the whole situation going right out of control.

'Let me *go*!' There was a thin note of hysteria in her cry. She was desperate and determined to get away from him because he was so dangerous.

For some reason Quinn laughed, a harsh sound without humour. 'What a foolish thing to do, Nicole!'

She tried to release her hand, but he only held it tighter. 'You're hurting me!' Her young breasts outlined against the thin cream chiffon rose and fell in agitation.

'It's your own fault. In the first place, you really oughtn't to attack your host and in the second place you shouldn't be such a melodramatic little idiot.'

'If you want to hurt someone it's not going to be *me*!' She was so close to him she could see the fine, polished texture of his skin, the precise cut of his clearly defined mouth, the merciless blue eyes all the more startling against his black brows and lashes and the teak tan of his skin.

'How heroic!' Quinn spoke lightly and he even smiled. 'Isn't it too bad you've got the strength of a baby?'

'I could scream!' she muttered.

'For heaven's sake, I thought you were going to be sensible, not precipitate a scene.'

'Please let me go, Quinn!' The quick tears sprang into her eyes.

'Of all the emotional little fools——!' He let her go abruptly, his voice impatient and derisive. 'Anyone would think I was about to beat you or drag you away and throw you on my horse!'

'I'm sorry!' She was rubbing her wrist where dull red marks marred the white skin.

For an instant he watched her and his black brows drew together. 'What sort of a brute am I anyway?'

'A twinge of conscience?' She looked up at him a little shaken.

His expression was sombre and he reached out suddenly and took her wrist. 'I hate dealing with fragile little girls. It's maddening to have to kiss the hurt better!'

With his mouth on her wrist she was so shocked and disturbed she drew in her breath sharply, appalled and bemused by a wave of sensation. Her other hand lifted and for an instant hovered over his crisp dark head.

'Please, Quinn, I forgive you.'

'To my shame, little one, I wanted to hurt you!' He lifted his head and smiled at her, and she drew back, unendurably afraid. She was certain he could see his effect on her, the unbidden feelings he was arousing. What was wrong with her? Her heart was beating rapidly and she had to live with the shocked knowledge that if he chose to, despite her frail resistance, he could exploit her utterly. It was there in the brilliant eyes that regarded her so intently.

'I think my earache has gone.' She touched her delicate ear.

'I'm glad. You should be able to sleep now.'

'Will you turn the lights out?' she asked.

'I always do.'

The blue eyes seemed to be sparkling with mockery. 'Goodnight, Quinn,' she said with a little shiver of emotion in her voice.

'Shall I come up with you?'

His eyes seemed to be touching every part of her; her hair and her face and her tremulous body, so that for an instant she stood gazing at him like a girl in a trance.

'Well?' His tone was indulgent but just faintly cruel.

'I can easily find the way.' She had to blink her eyes to cut off the naked current. 'There are a few lights on in the gallery.'

'Poor little Nicole!' he said, and something in his expression set her free.

As she turned away from him her great dark eyes were glittering and she was filled with a sudden self-protectiveness. Though he made her feel weak and disorientated, her bitter experiences had removed from her all desire for emotional involvement. The best thing she could possibly do would be to stay out of Quinn Rossiter's way.

Two days later the girls were out riding when they saw the station's single-engined Piper Cherokee fly in over the property.

'That'll be Kim!' Christine exclaimed, and swept her blonde curls back under her hat. 'Let's ride back to the strip and meet him.'

'I'd love to!' Nicole had the certain feeling that Kim Rossiter wouldn't have the deep, dark depths of his stepbrother.

'Race you, then!'

'You're on!'

Both girls were good riders, light and easy in the

saddle, but gradually it became noticeable that Nicole had the edge over her friend despite her city upbringing. She drew away laughing, shouting encouragement to her flying mare, moving so smoothly and so beautifully it was a joy to ride her. An obstacle came up and instead of going round it, they went over it together, in one lovely motion like a polished performance, then galloped on hell for leather so that the birds flew away, shrill and angry at the disturbance, and the mare's hoofs scattered the gold and white daisies that swam in waves through the long grass.

Nicole was only a few yards away when she saw Quinn sitting his handsome black stallion in the shade of a large ghost gum. He was motionless watching her, so she checked the mare swiftly, pulling it in and slackening off pace so that Christine was able to move up alongside her.

'All right, you win. Hi there, Quinn. See the Piper come in?'

'I did.' Quinn answered his sister, then nodded at Nicole whom he hadn't seen at all that day. 'You ride beautifully, little one, but might I remind you it's a very hot day.'

'Is it?' She smiled at him and pushed the cream Stetson Christine had lent her off her head. She had drawn her shoulder-length dark hair into a Grecian knot, but a few tendrils had escaped to caress her cheeks and her nape. 'I haven't thanked you for allowing me to ride this beauty while I'm here!' She drew her hand lovingly down the bay's satin neck.

'Once I saw you could,' he pointed out dryly. 'I still don't think I believe it!'

'She can beat me!' Christine looked pleased at her friend's accomplishment. 'Are you coming down to meet Kim?'

'What do you think? Margot's flown back with him. And Wayne.'

'You mean it?' Christine looked dismayed.

'Don't you want to see your cousins?'

Christine's light blue eyes were unsmiling. 'Some of them. What's wrong with Wayne now?'

'He's the only one who could tell you that. Let's ride!'

Christine stared at her stepbrother thoughtfully, then when he looked back at them, both girls reined in alongside the big black stallion. 'Cousin Matt, that's Margot's and Wayne's father, runs Willunga for us,' Christine explained to her friend. 'Matt's a dear, we're all very fond of him, but Wayne isn't the tower of strength he should be to his father. He takes no real interest in station affairs and he spends a lot of his time in the city.'

'I suppose the Outback isn't everyone's life,' Nicole observed, trying to speak fairly.

'So it isn't, but Wayne shouldn't let poor old Matt support him. Margo too. She's a great one for the good life.'

'She does a damn sight more than Wayne any day!'

'What about it?' Christine kept her eyes on her stepbrother's dark profile. 'My guess is she's trying to be a lot closer than a cousin.'

'Kim's been spoken for!'

'Who's talking about Kim?' Christine asked satirically. 'Think that, brother, and you'll be making a fatal mistake.'

'Have I made one so far?' he spoke as coolly as Christine was heated.

'You've never needed diagrams in your life. Margot's devotion to you is all very touching, but——'

'Forget it!' Quinn said simply. 'Would you bind me to a woman like ... Nicole, for instance?'

'If you ask me, she'd be perfect!'

'Romantically, certainly. It would be easy to make love to her.'

'Why don't you ask me?' Nicole broke in spiritedly. 'I don't think I would even *want* to add up to your exacting standards.'

'What did she say?' Quinn asked his sister dryly, though he spoke to Nicole with his eyes.

'It's simple enough. She says she's not for you.'

'We both know that!'

Nicole caught her breath in earnest. 'Beast!'

'You've already told me that.'

'Oh, when?' Christine's blue eyes grew bright and alert.

'Nicole may find it convenient to forget,' he shrugged.

'Look, Kim's landed!' Nicole shaded her eyes with her hand.

'There was nothing I wanted more than for Mother and me to have you all to ourselves, now Margot and Wayne arrive!' said Christine, still recovering from the shock.

'Would you have had me say no?' Quinn grasped her fingers.

'Too bad you're so decent,' she told him. 'Mark my words, Margot won't rest until she's your fiancée.'

'Just the same we'd better go and say hello to her!' Quinn silenced her dryly. 'Wayne will probably believe the angels sent Nicole for his delight.'

'Thanks a million!' said Nicole, and charged after Christine who had suddenly gone at a dash across the open, sunlit flat.

By the time they had all dismounted and tethered the horses Kim and one of the station hands had unloaded some boxes and two pieces of luggage. 'Come and meet Kim!' said Christine, and grabbed her friend's hand. 'You'll see what I mean about Margot and Wayne. She's madly in love with Quinn, and she always has been.'

Nicole digested that piece of information without speaking. Poor Margot! She had it in her to feel sorry for the girl.

'It's Nicky, isn't it?' Kim had his hand outstretched, smiling.

'How are you, Kim. I'm very glad to meet you at long last.'

They shook hands and Nicole studied with pleasure Christine's younger brother. He was tall and boyishly lean with an attractive golden-skinned face and Christine's light blue, humour-filled eyes. Quinn came to join them and Nicole had no trouble detecting the hero-worship in Kim's smile. Margot and Wayne were in the picture now and Quinn took over and made the introductions as Nicole became aware she was under very close scrutiny from the Willunga Rossiters, sister and brother. Both were handsome in an unsmiling fashion, slightly patronising as though they could hardly bring themselves to speak to someone outside the family, though Nicole was conscious that Wayne Rossiter's jaded hazel eyes changed ever so slightly.

'Whose idea was it to come?' Margot spoke directly to Nicole as soon as the men had turned away for a moment.

'What on earth does that matter?' Christine interjected. 'I asked Nick, as it happened.'

Margot's grey, green-flecked eyes were still studying Nicole intently. 'I know you from some place, don't I?'

'Nicole had to slip away from a great career,' Christine explained. 'She's a pianist. Perhaps you've seen her perform?'

'Really?' Margot looked taken aback.

'Chris is joking,' Nicole said quietly, vaguely upset by Margot's manner. 'I'm sure we haven't met before, Miss Rossiter, I should remember.'

'Nevertheless I seem to know your face.' Margot's eyes were sharp and questioning again. 'Where do you come from? What do you do?'

'What is this, the third degree?' Christine put in indignantly. 'Nicole is my friend, a guest on Sapphire, not one of the hands you employ.'

'I'm sorry,' Margot raised fine, arched eyebrows, drawling her words, 'if your friend doesn't really like answering questions.'

'Boy, are you a cold shower!' Christine retorted, and she wasn't joking.

Margot's long hazel eyes didn't waver. 'Have I offended you, Miss Lindfield?'

'Not at all,' Nicole said pleasantly, thinking the charge was only a hair's breath away. 'Christine and I are old friends from our uni days. I always planned on visiting her, now I'm here.'

'Have you a job or anything at home waiting for you?' Margot asked.

'No, I'm quite free to enjoy myself,' Nicole smiled back at her.

'Lucky girl, I'm always flat out!' Margot retorted in her smooth drawl, and looked back towards the men. 'You'll excuse me, won't you? I must tell Quinn something before I forget.'

'Phew!' Christine whistled under her breath. 'She doesn't like you.'

'I can see that.'

'Jealous, of course!' Christine almost smiled. 'Don't take any notice of her, sweetie. Margot always leaves her manners behind when she's dealing with her own sex. She's very careful with Mamma, respectful in all things, but it doesn't take half an eye to see it's all calculation. The only person she cares about in this world outside herself is Quinn.'

'She's very good-looking,' Nicole murmured, making a few observations of her own.

'And she knows it!' Christine muttered in a tone of annoyance. 'I couldn't bear to have her a closer relative than she is now. Isn't it wonderful the way she's smiling at Quinn? I've never seen her smiling at anyone else like that in my whole life. I've known her to be really mean to anyone who shows an interest in him.'

'And what does Quinn have to say?' Nicole asked, finding it unexpectedly jarring to see Margot's tall, slim figure ranged alongside Quinn's, the long elegant face raised to his, the sun on her dark chestnut hair.

'Quinn is renowned for playing a close hand. No one really knows what he thinks about Margot. You have to remember she's an entirely different person with him and she's got lots of ability when she cares to use it. She knows all about running a big station, stock holding, book work, the lot. She's not beautiful like you or even the kind of woman other women like, but she can look very striking, she can grace the head of the table and she can handle staff. In a lot of ways she's the kind of woman Quinn needs—even I can see that. Whenever she's here, they really get along very well, or they seem to. She follows him round everywhere—you know, *learning*. Quinn's the expert. He has the final say on everything, even on Willunga. Cousin Matt is a good man and I hate to say it, but he's made a few miscalculations. I suppose that's what Margot is here to talk about.'

'And her brother?' Nicole was conscious that Wayne Rossiter had sent several narrowed glances in her direction.

'Oh, yes, Wayne,' Christine answered flatly. 'Wayne is quite different. I even feel sorry for him in a way. Margot loves her world. She's a born countrywoman, efficient and self-contained, but Wayne is unexpectedly arty. He likes to paint, and it's no use shooting him down.'

'I wasn't going to.' Nicole moved back a little into the shade, her eyes ranging over the small group near the hangar. 'It must be difficult for him when he's expected to be a cattle baron.'

'He could never be that!' Christine bit off a little contemptuously. 'He just hasn't got the guts to get out and make it on his own, so he wants to make it on the art scene. So why doesn't he? He's got real ability, but he's got too darned used to being supported in style. Poor old Matt can't understand him any more than Wayne can understand his father, but he lets his father pay and pay all the way. Soon there won't be any strength left in Matt at all. Aunty May was drowned in a flash flood about three years ago. She kept the whole family together.'

'How sad!' said Nicole, feeling a little weight on her heart at the news. 'I suppose there are all kinds of dangers I don't know about.'

'Fire, flood, drought, day in and day out anxieties that make a man weaken. It can be a very lonely life without family and the right partner.'

'I can understand that very well,' Nicole nodded slowly. 'Does Quinn ever speak of his mother?'

'Never!' said Christine, after a pause. 'I never say he's my *step*brother. I never like to, I love him so much. Val and Kim are the same. Mother always makes the distinction because she feels she has to. I mean, everyone for thousands of miles around knows the old story. As a very young man Dad brought out a beautiful bride of good family and a name you would recognise if I told you, but it didn't work out. Quinn's mother couldn't take it. To love her husband and later her baby son wasn't enough. In some ways it's only the veneer of civilisation out here. You're very close to fundamentals, living and dying and the power of the land. We've had drought here, when it's been really bad, and we've had the good seasons as well when it doesn't seem possible so much beauty could exist. It's all a question of being at peace or at war with your environment. Quinn's mother broke under the strain. My father was a rather solitary man and of course he had tremendous pressures on him as head of the whole clan and responsible for balancing the ledgers. Other family holdings have broken up, but somehow the Rossiters hold on. My uncles are good cattle men, good business men, but they all lean on Quinn. When he marries, believe me, he won't make any mistakes. It has to be a woman of our own world or a woman who would make Quinn—Sapphire—her whole life. They're one and the same!'

CHAPTER FOUR

FOR the rest of the day Margot appeared to apply herself eagerly towards proving that she was indeed Quinn's kind of woman, then in the evening, after striding around the property, or standing close to him in the office, she miraculously blossomed into Woman, her slim figure sheathed in slinky jersey, her hair curled, the full battery of evening make-up and trailing a rich, long-lingering fragrance.

If Quinn didn't appear fascinated he wasn't looking away from her either. He presided at the head of the dinner table, more relaxed than Nicole had ever seen him, parrying Margot's little feminine thrusts easily, being charming and attentive to Helen, looking down the table at all of them, leading the topics of conversation and drawing them all into them. All in all, they covered a lot of ground and revealed facets of his personality and interests that Nicole wasn't aware of. For instance, painting. There was a wonderful collection of paintings right through the house, including Australian masterpieces Nicole had seen reproduced, but Quinn was obviously knowledgeable about the fresh, young moderns. He even succeeded in bringing the rather withdrawn and aloof Wayne to life with his talk of the exciting new wave of young artists, including a young man called Jeremy Roland, who had stayed on Sapphire for six months, working and painting the remarkable colours and light of the Outback.

'You mean he still writes to you?' Wayne was saying, in his soft, cultured drawl.

'Why, certainly.' Quinn looked directly at his cousin. 'I value our correspondence. Jem wasn't much of a jackeroo despite his enormous energy, but no one could deny his talent. He's having a one-man showing next month at the Ekert Gallery in Adelaide and he wants us to be there. Several of his best works were painted right here on Sapphire—at least that's what he tells me.'

'I bet *Desert Silence* is one of them,' Christine said happily, 'and *Early Morning on Sapphire*. I wish you'd met him,' she smiled at Nicole across the table. 'He fell off a horse so many times it was painful to watch him, but as soon as he picked up a paintbrush, it was magic. After a while, Quinn just let him paint.'

'Was that good business?' Margot smiled.

'It was peaceful!' Quinn's shapely mouth curved in amused remembrance.

'I wish to God someone would let *me* do that!' Wayne muttered intensely, patches of colour appearing on his prominent cheekbones. 'Paint—that's all I've ever wanted to do.'

'Then why don't you?' Quinn said crisply, and refilled Margot's wine glass.

'I think you know why!' Wayne returned low-voiced.

'One thing's sure, Matt can't go it alone. He needs help!' Kim protested.

'He has *me*,' Margot pointed out, turning her head.

'I'm sure he's deeply grateful!' Kim gave a little bow. 'The trouble is, Wayne, you won't make your position clear.'

'Certainly not at the dinner table!' Quinn made it clear they were to keep to pleasantries. 'There are a few things I intend to point out, but that will keep until to-morrow. Running a major industry isn't easy and clearly Matt can't get over May's tragic death. I think he needs a holiday, a long holiday—halfway across the world, for that matter. He needs a complete change of scene. I should have seen to it before, but I knew he wouldn't go.'

'That's it, Quinn!' Helen said softly. 'I agree with you.'

'But, dear heaven,' Margot's breath came rather hard, 'we simply couldn't manage. God knows I work hard enough now.'

'You seemed to stop when I arrived!' Kim observed dryly.

'Let's say I was entitled to!' Margot flashed back a little heatedly.

'Now, children,' Quinn said gently, 'you'll find out what I propose tomorrow. Now,' he glanced up and smiled at Helen, 'I haven't much of a sweet tooth as you know, but whatever these are, they're delicious!'

'The girls made them.'

'Please—just Nick!' Christine held up a hand. 'No one could call her a spoiled female, she's a very accomplished young lady. I just sat there watching and gossiping and Mary did the dishes. What do you call them, Nicky?'

'Profiteroles. Chocolate-coated choux pastry filled with praline-flavoured whipped cream,' Nicole answered without hesitation. 'I'm glad you like them.'

'We do, indeed!' Kim took another one immediately.

'We're beginning to find out a lot about you that we never knew before.' Quinn's faint smile was rather wicked.

'I have a feeling—no, more than that, that I've seen Nicole somewhere before,' Margot said silkily, her deeply tanned skin gleaming in the light from the chandelier.

'Oh?' Quinn's voice held a slight edge. 'Where?'

'That's it!' Margot gave a little gurgling laugh. 'I don't know.'

'Probably she's on the ten most stunning females in the country list,' said Kim, leaning back in his chair and studying Nicole's downbent face. 'She sure fits the picture.'

'As a matter of fact,' Wayne said unexpectedly, 'that lily-white skin would be wonderful to paint!' As the overhead light was enhancing Margot's dark golden tan so it revealed the dazzling purity of Nicole's matt white complexion. Wayne was silent for a moment, then he asked bluntly: 'Have you ever had your portrait painted?'

'*Have* you?' Quinn's brilliant blue eyes had narrowed to pin points.

'Yes, I have.' Nicole looked back at him, seeing the faint sensual hostility in his face.

'I'd like to see it,' he said suavely.

'*I* have,' said Christine.

'Really?' Margot quickly rounded on her cousin. 'You've visited Nicole at her home.'

'Frequently!' Christine exaggerated. 'The portrait is outstanding—an excellent likeness, and more. You can look right into the eyes and see the real Nicole.'

'Oh, and who's that?' Margot raised her eyebrows, then smiled with hard eyes.

'I would say that's fairly obvious,' said Kim. 'You've still got to make your point, Wayne.'

Wayne looked down at his wine glass, then lifted his eyes to Nicole's face. 'You know, of course, that I paint?'

'Christine did mention it.' She was astounded to see that the thin, long-fingered hands were faintly trembling.

'Could you stand having your portrait painted again?' He spoke abruptly, in such a way that she knew if she laughed or said no she would somehow damage him.

'You mean you would like to?'

'A portrait to end all portraits,' Quinn added smoothly. 'Where and when is this all to take place?'

'I have a great idea!' Margot said brightly. 'Why

doesn't Nicole come back with us for a while? We'd love to have her and Wayne would be able to get on with the portrait.'

Christine sat bolt upright with her mouth open and Helen's small pretty hand fluttered, but before either of them could say anything Quinn dropped a brief and final: 'No!' into the silence.

'God bless you!' Christine breathed. 'We need Nicky right here.'

'Don't let 'em chase you away!' Kim turned his fair head to smile at Nicole so that she could feel her heart expand with sudden warmth.

'Don't be ridiculous, Kim!' Margot looked up sharply. 'It stands to reason Wayne will work best in his own studio.'

'Never mind that, Nick stays here!' Christine said quickly. 'She's my friend and she hasn't even begun her holiday.'

'I appreciate that!' Wayne looked down at his hands a little gloomily.

'Then the obvious answer is to fly what you need in,' Quinn said crisply. 'It's apparent you'd have a fight on your hands if you tried to take Nicole out. Anyway, I like nice little surprises for dessert.'

'So do I,' said Kim. 'You'd better give Mary the recipe.'

'She's already got it,' Nicole smiled. 'I don't want to keep my successes from the world.'

Later Wayne seized the opportunity to draw her out on to the veranda, convinced now that given the opportunity that he could produce a painting that would make his father look at it with admiration and wonderment. Wayne loved and respected his father and though he knew his father loved him, he had never believed in or even understood his artistic ability. One could show bafflement at an abstract, but a portrait of a beautiful young girl had its own wonderful eloquence.

As he spoke, Nicole sat silently, watching his elegantly chiselled profile. There was strain in the thin, handsome face, and the way he clasped his hands so tightly, and being naturally compassionate she attempted to draw him out.

'Forgive me, Wayne,' she asked with kindness, 'but do you feel guilty about your painting, as though it's wrong for you to want to paint instead of looking after the property?'

Wayne got to his feet and put out his hand. 'Let's walk a little way in the garden, shall we?'

'I'd like to, it's a beautiful night. I've never seen stars so big or so brilliant as I've seen here.'

'Yes,' Wayne agreed, without looking up at the fantastic celestial display. 'I can't even remember when I first started to draw. Mother always told me she just put a crayon in my hand and I was away. I've always believed in my own talent, so did Mother, but you're quite right, I do feel guilty. I love my father, but I'm not close to him like I was to my mother. If he had his way he would have changed us around. Margot loves the land, station life. She's absolutely splendid at mustering and cutting cattle and all the hundred and one jobs that I loathe. Then there's Quinn. We can't ever forget Quinn. We're the same age, yet he controls an empire and I'm obviously a failure. My father respects Quinn as if he was twenty years Dad's senior; I could even say he loves him like the son he never had. He's a strong, very vital man. None of us can match him. Margot has been madly in love with him since she was fifteen or sixteen and she's twenty-eight now and still waiting. At least she has the talents he needs.'

'And you don't feel anyone needs you?'

'If I could prove myself!' He turned to her in some

agitation. 'I've got to increase my stature in everyone's eyes; Dad's, Quinn's. Like a lot of strong men Quinn can afford to be magnanimous. He's never tried to make me feel weak or a fool, but he's so damned ... oh, you know, he has such *presence* he makes me feel utterly drained in contrast. Surely you think so too?'

'Not at all!' Nicole lied. 'You're just quite different, that's all. You wouldn't want to be a copy of Quinn?'

'It would suit Dad!' Wayne said with pent-up grimness on his face. 'I feel it's the greatest stroke of good fortune, call it fate, that we've met. The idea of painting you interests me immensely,' he went on. 'Not just because you have beautiful bones and your hair and your eyes contrast so strongly with that white magnolia skin, but there's sadness in you, and understanding. You feel for other people and it's apparent. You have very beautiful eyes and they look deeply. You're the first human being I've spoken to in a long while who's made me feel whole!'

He was holding her two hands and Nicole felt shocked and surprised by his vehement sincerity. 'I like you, too, Wayne,' she offered gravely, 'and if I can help you in your work I'll be very proud. I expect it will turn out beautifully. Christine told me you have a great deal of ability.'

'She did?'

'You speak as though you're surprised. She was quite enthusiastic, actually!'

'I've never thought she particularly liked me,' said Wayne with a painful smile.

'Perhaps you don't believe enough in yourself, Wayne,' Nicole told him quietly.

He started back from her, then bent his head and kissed her cheek. 'I think you've known a little grief and despair of your own?'

She didn't have to answer him, for Margot's voice rang out, taut and imperative:

'Wayne? Pa's calling from Willunga!'

Wayne drew an audible breath that was almost a hiss. 'I'd better go in.'

'All right. We'll talk again,' Nicole said gently.

'Yes, thank you.'

She watched him start back up the stairs, his handsome narrow head and his tall body outlined against the softly brilliant light from the hallway. 'Poor Wayne!' she thought, and gave an involuntary shudder. Something had bred in him an unhealthy self-contempt. She had not expected such insecurity and she felt deeply sorry for him. She sighed again and looked out over the garden. Probably he felt lost and abandoned after his mother died and what with being contrasted endlessly with Quinn since childhood. . . . It all seemed so destructive!

There was a strong scent of jasmine and boronia in the air and the great trees were absolutely still. Nicole tilted her chin to the stars glittering like great jewels against the velvety deep purple of the night sky. Some shone with a blue light, others yellow and red. The Southern Cross was brilliantly clear, the farthest star of the first magnitude, pointing to the South Pole. She had never been able to pick out the Cross so easily.

'Are you going to stay out here all night, brooding on the stars?'

She hadn't heard him and she swung around lightly, looking up into his eyes. 'You move very silently, Quinn!'

'You make it sound menacing,' he observed.

'It doesn't do anything for my composure!' She tilted her head away and looked back at the stars. 'I've never seen anything like this glittering display.'

'Oh, was that what Wayne was doing? Naming off the constellations?'

'No. He was just telling me a little about himself.'

'His painting, for instance? How no one understands him?'

In the soft glow of the stars, her face was like a pearl, her eyes extraordinarily dark and deep. 'He didn't bore me in the least.'

'Go on!' He took her elbow as if she was just another one of his possessions leading her further out of the light that rayed out from the house.

She said stiffly, 'Our conversation was confidential.'

'I don't think that's a very good idea. You're not looking for more trouble, are you?'

'How can you say that?' she protested.

'Don't play dumb, little one. I happen to know you're a very intelligent girl even if you do invite disaster. Did you know, by the way, that the Southern Cross was once visible to the people of ancient Babylonia and Greece?'

'No, I didn't!'

'Yes,' he continued, mock-conversationally, 'they considered it part of the constellation Centaurus. Over the many centuries the Cross has gradually shifted southward in the sky. Surely you should have picked up that piece of information at your famous girls' school? Despite herself Nicole jerked a little away from him and he tightened the hold on her arm. 'Berkley, wasn't it?'

'Chris told you.'

'Why are you whispering?' He swung her to face him, his eyes a silvery shimmer.

'I'm naturally reluctant to shout. You seem to be a past master at backtracking.'

'Actually I encouraged Chris to fall into the trap,' he told her. 'It was out before she knew it. Don't you want me to know where you went to school?'

'I'm flattered by your interest,' she shrugged.

Quinn released her and began to whistle under his breath. 'What was Wayne's story?'

'He needs help!' she said a little fiercely for one so gentle.

'You saw that, did you?'

'Basically he's been pushed into the wrong mould.'

'Did he say who did the pushing?' he asked so dryly she couldn't conquer the impulse in time.

'You must know the answer to that one!'

'Ah, yes, I thought I'd come into it!' He gave a short brittle laugh. 'Don't you think Wayne's clung to his dilemma too long? He's not a boy finding his way. He's thirty-two years old. It always startles him, I know.'

The suave, cutting voice made her feel wretched. 'Not everyone can rise to the challenge of greatness,' she said jerkily.

'It seems some men are able to draw deeply on your compassion,' he observed. 'I suppose it's inevitable Wayne is one of them. I'm not trying to be cruel, but I believe he's incurably second-rate. He's been given plenty of chances to prove himself. Young Jeremy Roland who was here is fighting his way to the top, and he's a boy who started life as an orphan. It's a bitter fact Wayne lacks the stuff that transcends obstacles. It's bad enough that we've all had to listen to him, now I can see him clinging to you with the same tenacity as he clung to his mother. May should have been more honest with him, and I think she lamented it to her dying day.'

'The fact remains that he's desperately unhappy!' Nicole could feel herself trembling.

'Oh, be quiet!' he cut her off brutally. 'I should have stopped this from the start, now Wayne's all set to produce a masterpiece.'

'Don't you want him to?'

'Come again?' he said tautly, his arrogant dark head lifting like some mettlesome thoroughbred.

'I wonder if you want him to succeed?' she cried urgently.

'That's all I need from you!' His hand closed over her shoulder and she broke away frantically, turning on her heel and running across the lawn like a frightened child.

Her heart was pounding in her breast, the thick fall of her hair sliding across her face, when a black shape flew right at her from the enveloping trees. She recoiled and cried out, her hands coming up to shield her face. She was whimpering when Quinn pulled her into his arms.

'Oh, dear, more screaming?'

'What was it?' Her head fell forward against his hard chest.

'Just a poor little flying fox trying to find a fruit tree. They have very poor vision, as you know.'

'Yes.' For an instant she couldn't move, but surrendered to the sweet torment of his male strength. 'You must have a fine opinion of me?'

'You don't seem to be able to walk around by yourself in perfect safety.'

With a sense of shock Nicole realised her cheek was against the soft cloth of his shirt, her hair warm and scented beneath his chin. How could she hate him when he was easing some ache inside her? The thought stabbed her and the next moment she pulled away from him.

'I'm sorry if I said the wrong thing back there.'

'No doubt you'll do it time and time again.'

'You won't help me, will you?' she said a little plaintively.

'You can't win 'em all! But a word of advice before we go in. If I were you, I'd be very careful with Wayne. Be sympathetic if you must, but for God's sake don't play up to him.'

'Playing up to men was never my forte!' she said with a little despairing sigh.

'Damn it, little one, I remain unconvinced!' His brilliant, brooding glance slid over her. 'Where is your ex-fiancé now?'

It hit her hard, so hard, her eyes filled with tears and again she felt the endless, bottomless guilt.

'You tragic little fool!' He spoke harshly, lifting her chin and conquering the urge to shake some sense into her. 'Who broke it off, you or him?'

'I did.' The muscles of her throat were knotting, so it came out in a husky whisper.

'And it's too much to hope for you to forget him?'

'*Please*, Quinn!' Her expression suggested he was torturing her.

'So you can't talk about it?'

'No.' It came out low and piteous.

'Then do you mind if I say you're a plain damned fool!'

'You knew that when we met!' Nicole said just as violently.

'So I did!' He stared at her incredulously, looking down into her drowning eyes, then impatiently he brought up his hand and flicked a tear from the poignant curve of her cheek. 'Don't you think you owe it to yourself to get more perspective on the problem?'

'I can't shut him out!' She shook her head despairingly. 'Don't you think I've tried?'

'All right!' He suddenly put his arm around her, as indulgent as an older brother. 'Let's go down and see Midnight's foal. Six or seven months isn't such a long time anyway. Young girls change their minds every day.'

She tried to smile and by the time they reached the stables complex she was pale but composed. 'You can be kind sometimes, can't you?' she said.

'Don't count on it, flower face!' He smiled rather tightly and she could see the familiar mockery in his eyes.

As soon as Quinn turned on the light, Midnight turned

her head around, her ears pricked, enquiring, alert and watching over her day-old foal. 'Hi, girl!' Quinn said easily, giving the mare a moment to get used to the sight of them, then he moved forward to run his hand over Midnight's satin flank. The mare's ears moved gently and Quinn slid his hand over her neck while Nicole approached the little foal.

'Isn't he beautiful?' Her colour had brightened. 'Hi, Midnight!' Her voice was low and musical as she spoke to the standing mare. 'You must be very proud of your handsome son!'

'Of course she is!' said Quinn, and laughed as the mare snorted and arched her neck. 'Steady, beautiful! It wasn't quite as easy as you're making out.'

'But isn't he a lovely boy?' Nicole murmured, 'even if he was trying to come the wrong way.' The foal, a bright bay colt with a star on its forehead, still lay at its mother's feet, but it twitched its endearing, long spindle legs and opened its soft, oval-shaped eyes.

'You're awake, are you?' Quinn bent down beside Nicole and ran a loving, calming hand over the little foal.

'What a refined little head!' Nicole commented, her expression tender. 'I love all animals, but I have a special feeling for horses.'

'I can see that!' Quinn moved slightly so she could better caress the beautiful, innocent little creature.

'What are you going to call him?' she asked.

'How about Noonfire?'

'I like that.' She turned her head to smile at him, unaware that her whole expression had softened magically and there was even gaiety in the curve of her lovely mouth.

'Well!' he said dryly, and his brilliant eyes narrowed over her. 'Well, well, well!'

'What is it?' She sank back on her heels.

'Just for a moment, for the first time, you were actually yourself.'

'Oh?' She just looked back at him, uncertain what to say.

'Beautiful, glowing, carefree, perhaps a little too beautiful!' He put out his hand and wound a thick strand of her hair round his finger. 'Silk!' he said, as though he was faintly irritated with himself for noticing.

Nicole said nothing, did nothing for the sheer want of strength to pull away. There was a strange panic in her body, a vulnerability that filled her with an anguish she had never known before. Peter had never aroused in her this terrible physical confusion. She was sure the heat that was now inside her was colouring her skin.

'Quinn?' It came out very soft and anxious. 'Shouldn't we be going back now?'

He still held the black skein of her hair and tugged it a little painfully. 'What are you afraid of, some kind of violence?'

There was passion in his dark face as well as a hard strength, the kind of high handed masterfulness that could sweep a woman along and leave her wide open to a tidal wave of emotion.

'No!' She said it too quickly, trembling with nervousness. 'I just mean the others will be wondering where we are.'

'Is that all?' His blue eyes frankly mocked her.

'Yes.' She tilted her head back so that the skein of her hair was pulled tight. 'Oh!' she gave a little involuntary whimper.

'You did it to yourself!' His tone was ironic, deepening dangerously. Nicole closed her eyes, trying not to respond to him, when footsteps clattered outside on the stone paving.

'Quinn?'

The voice they heard was Margot's and it sounded faintly breathless as if she had been running.

'Open your eyes, Nicole,' said Quinn in an amused drawl, 'the cavalry has arrived!'

'I think I'm glad!'

'I'm sure you are.' He drew her to her feet just as Margot called again in high-pitched entreaty:

'Quinn, where are you?'

'Do you want to go out the back way?' Quinn asked suggestively, but there was amusement in his attitude.

'Perhaps Margot will think I've been egging you on?' Nicole found herself answering tartly.

'Good God!' he smiled at her and the air was charged with devilry and challenge.

'*Quinn!*' This time it was almost a shout and much closer, so Quinn went to the door and looked out into the darkness.

'Here, Margot!' he called casually, and Nicole found herself laughing because it seemed so ridiculous.

'Where the devil have you been? What happened?' Margot ran almost awkwardly right up to the stable door.

'Happened?' Quinn glanced down at her in such a way she flushed. 'Surely our being here is quite accountable?'

'Is there something wrong with the colt?' Margot's sharp tone had lost its attack.

'No, he's quite healthy and contented.' Quinn straightened up nonchalantly. 'Come in and see.'

Margot pushed past him, not even glancing at the mare or the lovable little foal with its large startled eyes. 'Oh, there you are, Nicole. Wayne was looking for you,' she added crisply, her hazel eyes snapping and her skin glowing with colour from her recent exertions.

Nicole smiled back at her, her own heightened emotions sensing Margot's deep tension. 'Is that an order?' she asked pleasantly.

Margot shook her head. 'Aren't you concerned about your portrait?'

'There's plenty of time to make arrangements.'

'That's very true!' Quinn said as though he wanted to irritate both of them. Margot was looking insulted, and Nicole, falsely dreamy, the light shining full on her white skin and the loose sweep of her hair.

The mare snickered and Quinn turned to reassure her. 'I'm afraid we're disturbing Midnight. We'd better go.'

Nicole agreed. She bent down to stroke the foal again, then she straightened and walked to the door. 'I think I can find my own way.'

'Oh, good.' Margot's yellow flecked eyes were very hard and cold. 'It's my turn for a breath of fresh air.'

Her hostility hit Nicole forcibly, but in the instant she turned away like a doe poised for flight Quinn spoke to her almost curtly.

'Just a moment, Nicole. Why should you rush on ahead? You're among friends.'

He was looking towards her so he didn't see Margot's malignant expression or the way two dull spots of colour broke out over her strong cheekbones, but Nicole registered everything with startling clarity. Rumour had it Margot was mean to anyone who so much as glanced at Quinn with desire, but so far as Nicole was concerned, Margot could become murderous when presented with a real threat. Her experience at the hands of Peter's mother had been bad enough, and in that moment she saw disaster in Margot's hostility. Such women were destructive; vain and possessive and violently jealous.

Quinn's voice seemed to come to her from a distance. In spite of his clear order for her to accompany them, she turned on her heel and ran lightly along the flat stretch of paving, then out on to the velvety soft grass. Margot was welcome to her dynamic cousin. Let Margot pander to his moods and complexities, the uncompromising maleness, the merciless physical radiance. Quinn Rossiter could only give a woman hell. She was glad now, *glad*, that she was quite out of his reach. What else were cruel experiences for but to teach? She was sure now she had never loved Peter and just as equally convinced it would be agony to develop a mad obsession for the owner of Sapphire.

She was almost but not quite at the house before she realised Margot might have interpreted her flight as the uncontrollable reaction of the guilty, instead of the deep desire not to be drawn further. If so, the whole incident took on a nightmarish quality. She had been gazing directly into Margot's eyes and she had seen the look of total enmity.

When she saw Christine standing on the veranda she slowed down and flung back her wind-tossed hair, half blinded now by the sudden spill of light. 'I've just dropped in on Midnight and the foal. It's adorable!'

She was hot now and shaken, so she gathered up her long hair and held it on top of her head, the skin of her arms and her throat and her face flawlessly white.

'Well, come in now,' Christine was laughing and unsuspecting. 'Mother has pulled out all the old photographs of the lot of us at all ages. I want you to see them.'

'I'd love to!' Swallowing her confusion, Nicole linked her arm through her friend's and together they walked back into the house.

CHAPTER FIVE

Over breakfast the next morning Christine suggested they take the horses and ride out to the hill country where Paddy, the young tracker-stockman, had first found the tektites, the 'black diamonds' from Heaven. Quinn kept them in a drawer in his office and he had shown them to Nicole the night before. Black, glassy and lustrous, they appeared to Nicole like teardrops, and the most advanced scientific theory was that they had come from the moon. Tektites had struck earth in showers aeons of time ago, but as far as it was known, they had only been discovered in nine locations around the world. But while scientists puzzled about these glassy meteorites, the Australian aboriginals had been using the black diamonds as ammunition for their slings. Paddy had been quite complacent about his discovery and stood dumbfounded while Quinn took them off him and locked them in his office. Such unique little stones were too interesting to give to the children to play with like marbles, which in fact Quinn later supplied to Paddy's three little sisters and brothers as a very welcome consolation prize.

While Christine propounded a fantastic theory of her own, Wayne sat stirring his coffee and staring down at it as though he was convinced a poisonous chemical had been added, or so it appeared to Nicole who had been watching him. There were only four of them at the table. Quinn and Kim had had breakfast at first light and this morning Helen concluded a little dryly that Margot must have joined them because she was nowhere to be found. Later, when Mary their housekeeper came in with the hot dishes, she confirmed that Miss Margot had indeed been up early, fretting to get out and join the men at the camp draft.

It occurred to Nicole that Wayne should have offered to join them, but an hour later as they rode through the citrus orchard she could see that at least he was an excellent horseman. Christine had been perplexed and disconcerted by his determination to ride along with them, but after a while, because the morning was so beautiful and the day stretched before them, her attitude began to soften, and they all rode companionably side by side.

As always, the immensity of the land had an hypnotic effect on Nicole. The great plains ran away to the incredibly blue sky while much farther to the west were the great red sandhills on the edge of the waterless desert; unfamiliar, lonely parts of the run where the women weren't allowed without guides. A light breeze was blowing, turning the glittering silver windmills where the mobs could drink at the sub-artesian bores. As they rode Christine pointed out all the areas of interest, the lignum swamps and the waterholes with their great concentration of birds, the sacred places, the taboo places where the native boys quivered with fear, the favourite sites for thanksgiving dances and corroborees, the camp where the brolgas had come in early one morning and performed their magical ballet.

Ahead of them was the hill country with its shrub-shrouded caves, dingo lairs and homes for the kangaroos and the wallabies. There were fine cave drawings too that were rigorously protected, and search as they might no one could find them except the family and all the aborigines on the property, who regarded the caves and the ancient drawings as sacred. Bird cries followed them everywhere, great flights of them that Nicole was beginning to recognise. The budgerigars were unmistakable, flashing slantwise in a solid band of bright green, twittering and chittering, so Nicole sat on her horse and looked up at them with delight.

'You can't know how much I want to start sketching you!' said Wayne, in a strangely urgent voice. 'Your changing expressions are remarkable. You really love it here, don't you?'

'Don't *you*?' She looked away from the myriad little birds and waited for his answer.

'No.'

'I don't believe it!' Nicole replied. 'You're an artist. You must be susceptible to beauty in all its forms.'

'Aren't you forgetting I've seen this all my life?' Wayne muttered tersely as though he were trying to tell her something important. 'It's too harsh for me, too lonely. You can't really know what it's like. The dry is too dry and the wet is too wet and there's always the fear of famine or flood. Nothing's simple, or easy. I love horses but I have no interest in cattle at all. Or sheep. I'm proud of the Rossiter heritage, of course, but sometimes I find the isolated life unbearable. I'm not alone either—not in this family. Quinn's mother couldn't take it either. I expect you know the story?'

'We don't usually talk about it!' Christine pointed out a little tartly. 'I don't enjoy the way you're always pointing out that Quinn is my stepbrother.'

Wayne ignored her, watching Nicole narrowly with his sister's long hazel eyes. 'A city girl wouldn't stand a chance with Quinn!'

'What nonsense!' Christine said in a choked tone.

'Not nonsense at all, as you very well know.' Wayne offered his cousin a pitying smile. 'You'll listen, Nicole, won't you? A lot of girls have broken their hearts over Quinn.'

'Margot's been after his scalp a long time!' Christine said so loudly she startled her mount.

'Will you stop shouting?' Wayne asked mildly. 'Margot can take anything Quinn hands out. She's mad about him, we all know that. I bet it's no surprise to Nicole. Next to Quinn there's nothing Margot wants more than Sapphire.'

'Suppose you remember this is *my* home!' Christine snapped, and her slight shoulders seemed to slump under a weight.

'I'm sorry, Chris!' Wayne's voice sounded kind. 'But you must expect it. Quinn and Margot would make a good match. You know yourself he's passed over all the society butterflies. He was bitterly disillusioned as a boy and he's never forgotten it. Quinn won't make the same fatal mistake his father did. It's Margot, all right. He's sure of her, but he's still subjecting her to a trial before he finally takes pity on her and marries her.'

'Shall we ride on?' Christine suggested in a blank tone.

'Let's do!' Nicole leaned over and patted her friend's hand. 'I'm so enjoying myself.'

'So was I until Wayne started confiding his hopes!'

'You must see you're a very possessive little sister!' Wayne pressed his charge quickly and with a certain malicious satisfaction.

'Maybe I am,' Christine returned with a great effort. 'It will take us another hour to get to the top of the mesa. We'll have lunch there.'

'Perfect!' Nicole said brightly, hoping that a truce could be arranged between the cousins. Despite her usual warm tolerance, it was apparent that Christine came down hard on her cousin. She even allowed an edge of contempt to flash out here and there. Nicole was surprised by the way Christine and Wayne were constantly measuring each other. She had been made well aware of

it the previous night when neither of them seemed able
to resist the temptation to take a shot at the other. In a
way they were antagonistic, and she wondered why. After
all, Christine should have been able to shrug off Wayne's
inability to make a name for himself either as a cattle
baron or an artist. It was sad and it was a waste, but
surely it shouldn't arouse Christine to a banked fury?
They weren't brother and sister, or even close cousins,
yet Christine allowed Wayne to upset her deeply; Nicole
could see that now, and it had to have a meaning. Christine looked on Wayne as a hopeless case when it seemed
that underneath she really wanted to be proud of him.

Perhaps they were a lot closer than Nicole had ever
supposed. She had been on Sapphire for such a short time
she knew little else than she loved it. Born and raised in
a big city, she wasn't really dependent on an urban background. All this stark beauty, the wonderful historic
homestead, more than made up for the isolation that
Wayne seemed to find so unbearable.

Happily the next few hours floated along on a tide of
discovery for Nicole, at least. They came upon kangaroos and wallabies, but not the tip of a dingo's tail. The
dingoes were immensely cunning and though they were
there, they kept well out of sight as the horses picked
their way delicately over the stony ground. They came
upon snakes too, and giant lizards sunning themselves on
rocks, and if Nicole quivered nervously Christine and
Wayne rode on by with a nonchalance Nicole found impressive.

Lunch was simple and satisfying, but when they
emerged from the last of the three sacred caves covered
in primitive scenes and symbols, the sky was piled up
with livid colour. It was Nicole's introduction to the sudden and spectacular thunderstorms that rolled across the
heavens from nowhere. Before they reached flat ground

they heard the crack of thunder and the air was so still and hot the feathery stands of acacias were quivering in a silvery-blue sea of mirage.

Christine pointed up to the sky where the great storm-clouds were rimmed with strange lights. 'Spectacular, isn't it, but it mightn't mean anything. We've had thunderclouds for weeks at a time without getting one drop of rain.'

'We'll take the short cut all the same,' Wayne decided, very firmly for him. 'It just could surprise us and tumble down.'

'Lovely!' Christine turned her golden-skinned face to the sky. 'A little rain will work miracles. All these flats, Nicky, will come alive with wildflowers and all the gullies will be filled. There's no more perfect garden than the desert after rain. Paper daisies cover the sand like a carpet, the purple-flowering parakeelya that the stock can live on for months, the lilac Lambs' Tails and the green Pussy Tails that cover the hillsides in a sea of feathery plumes. After real rain the whole countryside, mile upon mile, is just a blaze of colour and scent. I want you to see it before you go home.'

'We've got quite a way to ride before we reach the homestead,' Wayne pointed out in a tone of concern. 'It won't be pleasant riding through the mud, and the horses don't like thunder.'

'Spoilsport!' Christine jeered. 'Let's see who gets there first!'

Christine took off on her bay gelding as though suddenly possessed of a great, almost uncontrollable restlessness and Wayne and Nicole after exchanging a solemn glance took after her. The horses all went hard as the light was diminishing, covering the ground with great strides so as to be free of the terror of the coming storm.

Nicole could feel her hair whip free, her blood was

singing and all her faculties were concentrated on getting into the lead. She had never realised it, but she had always shown the same reckless confidence on a horse. While the wind whipped and the thunder cracked she reacted with elation, almost relishing the possible danger. It was a side of her that at first seemed contrary to her gentle and sensitive nature, but she and the mare were one and at least for a little while she had back all her old nerve and pride.

They were coming towards the holding yards when the rain came down. Nicole felt the mare's momentary fear, but before it could take root in the animal's mind she was talking to it, conveying through voice and hands and heels that she was in control and together they would arrive home safely. When they came to a fence, she gave the mare no choice but to jump. It went for the solid obstacle at a fast, even gallop, lifting like a bird in a lovely fluid leap and clearing the top panel with ease.

'Oh, good girl, that was wonderful!' Nicole whispered jubilantly. It was a tremendous feeling to be going together so beautifully, a feeling of power, and on Nicole it acted like a drug. She had hardly time to wonder why Christine and Wayne weren't upon her, or whether one of them had taken a spill.

The fence cleared, she was uncertain now the quickest way back to the stables. Clearly she was in the lead and the rain was coming down heavily, drenching her silk shirt and plastering it to her body. Her hat too was gone, not that any of it seemed important. She felt vividly alive and she was damned if she was going to let them beat her even on their home ground.

Out of the green, spinning world the outline of a horse and rider materialised. Nicole's rain slicked face paled, then immediately suffused with colour. It was Quinn, and it was quite easy to pick out the big, dashing black

stallion. Even through the whirling rain she thought she
detected something violent in his attitude. Swiftly she
pulled the mare in and as Quinn closed in on them she
called out unsteadily:

'Have you seen Chris and Wayne?'

'No, I haven't!' His eyes were blazing blue and furious,
like he meant to skin her alive. 'What are you thinking of
travelling so dangerously fast?'

His anger jolted her, bringing a riotous reaction. 'I
know exactly what I'm doing!' she retorted deliberately,
adding fuel to the fire.

'No, ma'am!' He reached over and held the mare's
reins. 'You can do exactly what you like in the city, but
on Sapphire you'll listen to me. I don't want any needless
tragedies on this property and I want to send you home
in one piece.'

She drew in her breath sharply, her heart pounding and
her breath coming in gasps. 'You wanted to send me
home the minute you saw me!'

'Just give me the chance!' He sat the stallion with a
hateful arrogance she would have admired in another
man, the rain glistening on his bronzed skin and darkening the cream felt of his Stetson. 'In the saddle you put
yourself at risk. I've seen you with my own eyes.'

The rain was still falling, but neither of them seemed
aware of it, anger and urgency on the moist, verdant air.
She had to struggle to find the right words to lessen the
rising tension. '*Please*, Quinn,' she said tensely, 'I know
what I'm doing. The mare has good blood and she's
brave. You know your own horses. She's not afraid of
fences, and neither am I!'

'God help me, I know that!' he exploded. 'I even
understand it. The fact remains I've got trouble enough
without adding you to it. Who ever thought an iceberg
could act so wild? But then it's all an act, isn't it?'

A long-pent-up passion bubbled up in her and broke out of restraint. 'How *dare* you dictate to me!' she hurled at him, and the black stallion moved restively.

'Damn it, girl,' he quietened his powerful high-strung animal, 'you've got to learn control. Just watching you nearly scared me to death. You'll kill yourself one day, riding like that.'

'I'm telling you there was no reason to panic.'

'I'm not *asking* you!' He gave a hard, abrupt laugh. 'If the mare had refused the fence you'd have broken your neck.'

'Oh, nonsense, I'd have fallen off!'

'I'll be damned if I'm going to listen to you!' he returned violently. 'While you're on Sapphire, you'll do exactly as you're told.'

'O.K., I'll walk back!' Instantly Nicole dropped the reins, threw her leg over the pommel and slid to the ground. 'I'm not a fool or fainthearted, and it's no concern of yours if I *do* break my neck!'

Wretchedly she spun away from him towards the distant glimmering white outbuildings. All her joy and exuberance had dissolved in a hot burst of anger. Who did he think he was anyway, the king of the castle?

He caught her as she reached the first closed white bungalow, almost throwing her back against the vine covered wall. 'Don't touch me!' she cried breathlessly, suddenly afraid of him, his height and his strength cruelly accentuated.

'At least something can fire your blood!' he jerked her towards him, 'but lady, you've gone too far!'

'You don't frighten me!' The same reckless urgency that led her to high fences provoked her reply.

'We'll see!'

Her wet, slender body was burning in his arms, runnels of water sliding down their face and bodies, fusing their clothes to the skin. His hands were moving over her down her back and narrow waist, then as one arm still imprisoned her the other moved to hold her head where he wanted it, fingers twining into her thick, heavy ribbon of hair. It was impossible to twist or writhe in that hard expert grasp, but she tried a feeble blow.

'Easy!' he drawled mockingly, fending her off.

'You can't make a fool out of me!'

'No kidding!' He tilted her head back and as he lowered his head she cried out convulsively:

'I *hate* you!'

'It doesn't bother me!' His mouth curved in a smile and he wasted no more time but weighed down her mouth with his own, kissing her until she crumpled against him. There was no tenderness in his searching mouth, but passion and destruction, a hard dominance that made Nicole surrender up a part of herself she didn't even know existed. She had thought she had experience of love, of being made love to, but though Quinn was handling her deliberately, her reeling senses bore testimony to an excitement beyond anything she ever imagined.

There was hunger in him, she was sure of it, even as she was sure she wasn't trying to fight his physical hold over her. It was all happening so fast and it would haunt her for ever. The wind shook violently through the vines and tears mixed with the rain on her face. His mouth was travelling slowly down her throat, driving her crazy so that for a moment she felt giddy and fell completely against him while his mouth explored the white magnolia skin of her neck and her face. Finally he covered her mouth again, trapping her little moan of protest. Something irretrievable was being taken from her and she was frightened of such violent excitement, frightened of her own increasing abandonment.

With infinite control he released her, pressing her head back sharply into his arm. 'Look at me, Nicole,' he murmured tautly. 'I want to see if that fine blaze of spirit hasn't given way to tears.'

She had to cling to him to prevent herself from falling, but the aftermath of such wild emotion left her without a voice. She opened her eyes dazedly, burning black against her white skin, a high colour staining her cheekbones. The rain had stopped falling and above their heads was a patch of blue sky. For a while she stayed quiet, while he continued to look down at her upturned face, then she said hesitantly in a barely audible murmur,

'You're such a strange man. Such a very strange man!'

'But you're no stranger to me!' He brushed her parted mouth with the tip of his finger. 'Maybe next time for your own safety you won't feel so inclined to stir up a little action.' He relaxed the severity of his grip, holding her lightly as though aware of her weakness. 'Ah, Nicole,' he said dryly, a little bitterly somehow, 'the rain is over and so is our little storm in a teacup. One of these days you'll be going home, back to the hothouse where you belong. It's my responsibility to send you back in one piece. If you won't look after yourself, ₁ ll have to appoint someone to watch you.'

'Try it!' She stared up at him with her emotions in a turmoil.

'Don't worry, I will!'

Under the curt warning she thought she detected a real fear for her safety. She noticed his eyes were the same brilliant blue as the patch of sky, disconcertingly serious, and she supposed arrestingly beautiful with the thick, emphatic blue-black of his lashes.

'Surely you're not going to forbid me to ride?' she asked, suddenly robbed of hostility.

'I didn't say that!' Almost gently he pushed her wet,

shining hair behind her ear. 'I'm just determined not to allow you to take risks. Did you think I didn't know there was a tempest in you? I admire the way you ride, I even like your careless brilliance, but I think it would be best if you promised me now not to take any more chances.'

'I've been riding since childhood!' She gathered herself to stand away from his hard, handsome body.

'And I pray you'll be riding as an old lady!' He laughed briefly and tilted her chin. 'Take pity on me, little one. I'll let you do anything your heart desires, but I won't let you kill yourself.'

'Do you forbid Margot the high fences?' she asked guardedly.

Quinn didn't move for a minute, then his hand fell. 'I don't believe I've ever had occasion to discuss the matter!' His voice had altered and a frown appeared between his slanted brows. Abruptly he looked up at the rapidly clearing sky. 'Where the devil were you anyway?'

'I don't know. It must have been another life!' She felt detached from reality and it showed in her expression. She didn't know it, but she looked astonishingly beautiful, her dark eyes huge and velvety soft, her rose-coloured mouth faintly swollen, her rain-darkened hair falling away from the creamy whiteness of her skin.

'Try to remember!' he said, almost humorously.

A button had pulled away on her shirt and she was suddenly aware that the wet silk did little to conceal the shape of her breasts or the shadowed cleft. 'I shouldn't be here at all!' she said wildly. 'I should be looking for Chris and Wayne. We rode up to the hill country straight after breakfast and we only came down when we saw the stormclouds. Chris didn't think they would amount to anything. We decided to race back, and now I've missed them. I shouldn't be standing about. I should be *looking*!'

Quinn shook his head emphatically. 'Don't be ridiculous! I'll do the looking. You get on up to the house and take those wet clothes off.' His blue glance burned over her and though she wasn't in the least cold, she shivered violently.

When Quinn turned to whistle up the horses, they came instantly, the mare standing quietly while Nicole was given a leg up into the saddle. She sat loosely, giving the impression she could easily fall off.

'Are you all right?'

There was a sharp smile in his eyes that Nicole didn't like. 'Of course I am!' she said haughtily, immediately correcting her position. 'Why shouldn't I be?'

'At least you'll have no worries about staying on the shelf. Not if you can kiss like that!'

'Thank you!' She no longer felt the slightest desire to slouch. 'I've no intention of complicating my life.'

'Surely you already have, with at least one false start. You need a man, Nicole, someone with a lot more fire in him than your anonymous fiancé.'

'For God's sake!' She shook her head and would not permit herself to cry.

'Don't look so shocked, little one!'

'Am I to understand you're offering some release?' she said bitterly, hoping to silence him, but he only smiled, a white glimmer in an arrogant dark countenance.

'Not me, Magnolia,' he said in a pronounced drawl. 'I'm a solitary man!'

As Nicole found out when she arrived back at the homestead, Christine had taken a spill and was soaking her bruises in a hot bath. Wayne, white-faced and grim, had brought her in, then gone off himself to shower and change after having made certain Christine's injuries were indeed minor—as Christine later put it, 'mostly her pride'. With the mild disturbance in the household no one questioned Nicole closely, though they accepted her appearance with obvious relief, but when Quinn walked in ten minutes later checking everyone's whereabouts, it was immediately apparent that he knew which way Nicole had come and when she had reached the house.

Nicole was wrapped in her robe and drying her hair after a quick shampoo under the shower when Margot knocked on the door of her room.

'I hope I'm not disturbing you?' It was offered like a challenge and for a moment Nicole stood arrested, with her silky hair electric from the brush.

'Come in, Margot, and take a chair.'

'Thank you!' Margot's bright hazel eyes moved all-seeingly over Nicole's slender form and the perfectly beautiful satin robe. 'Was it a coincidence that you ran into Quinn?'

'I didn't see him at all until he loomed up in front of me.'

Margot nodded her head. 'I thought as much. He was quite angry when he came in.'

'Oh?' Nicole shrugged her shoulders. 'It could have nothing to do with me.'

'Of course Chris doesn't show any sense, galloping like that in the rain,' Margot added.

'Don't you?' Nicole couldn't help asking.

'What gallop in the rain? What the devil for?'

'Just the thrill of it.'

Margot's face altered subtly. 'My dear girl, I get all the thrills I can handle!' She glanced up at Nicole and laughed suggestively. 'No news to you, I suppose, that I feel somewhat exposed about my feeling for Quinn. Coming to Sapphire is like coming home, as it will be before long.'

'And just think, you won't even have to change your name.'

Margot looked sharply at Nicole's expressionless face as though questioning her wit. 'If you're lucky, dear, you may be privileged to attend our wedding.'

'Thank you. None of us are getting any younger. When is it to be?'

It was obvious Margot was making up her mind quickly, uncertain whether Nicole was being pleasant or not. Certainly her voice was sweet and gentle.

'Oh, in the New Year,' she said vaguely, and ran her left hand into the pocket of her skirt. 'Well now, tell me what you think about Wayne's offering to paint you?'

'I'm very flattered. I hope it turns out well for him.'

'What about *you*?' Margot smiled unpleasantly.

'It won't affect me at all,' Nicole answered quietly. 'I think you know too that Wayne is trying to prove something to himself. He's not a bred-in-the-bone cattleman like Quinn.'

Margot coloured hotly. 'Do you think I don't know that? Quinn loves the land more than he could ever love a woman. Some might think that strange, but I understand. Wayne has always needed a woman to lean on. It's very difficult to respect him even if he is one's own brother.'

'Perhaps he would be quite different in another environment?' Nicole offered candidly. 'Environmental influences are very important. They either drag one down or allow freedom to develop. Wayne is obviously artistic. Whether he's brilliant or not I don't know—I've seen nothing of his work.'

'And would you be able to make a valid judgment even if you did?' Margot asked with an air of disbelief.

'I think so. My father is a highly respected collector. I've been used to paintings all my life.'

'Really?' There was surprise in every inch of Margot's tall, rangy figure. 'It's very difficult to track your background down. What does your father do?'

He's a businessman. He holds a number of director-ships. You won't see his name mentioned often in the papers, and that's exactly the way he wants it.'

'Remarkable!' Margot's humourless mouth thinned. 'His daughter appears to be equally secretive. Even Chris is reticent about how your friendship flourished. What are you really out here for anyway? Girls like you are always after action and excitement. The Outback usually drives them mad.'

Nicole returned to brushing her hair. 'Doesn't that get back to what I was saying? Sapphire suits me very well. I must be an odd kind of city girl because I find it full of movement and adventure. The landscape is so big and bold, and while there's danger, there's peace!'

'*Peace?*' Margot laughed with an air of surprise. 'You're a little young to want peace, aren't you, or are you on the run from something or someone?'

'Is that any of your business in any case?' A sudden rush of anger loosened Nicole's tongue.

'I'm not sure!' Margot narrowed her long hazel eyes. 'No doubt you've got some nice young man at home to go back to, and I'd advise you to do just that. Or perhaps you're becoming interested in Quinn or Kim? Both have been spoken for.'

'How idiotic!' Nicole laughed with genuine amuse-ment. 'How can a man be spoken for, or a woman for that matter? You're either engaged to be married or you're not!'

Margot stood up quickly and her eyes sparkled with malice and dislike. 'Nevertheless, you'd be an absolute fool to look at either of them. Kim and Rosalind have been sweethearts for years and you're the last girl in the world Quinn would take seriously. Get Helen to show you the portrait of Marianne some time. Probably it's all covered in dust, but you might as well see it all the same. You and Marianne are much alike. Quinn's not a fool, he's a real man. He might admire a beautiful woman, a beautiful, *artificial* woman, but he could dispense with her too. He hates his mother—do you know that?'

'No!' Nicole shook her head. 'I haven't worked it out like you have, but I don't think hate is the word. It's not in keeping with his character. What hurt him he'd treat with a magnificent indifference.'

'You're very opinionated about Quinn!' Margot said ringingly. 'How have you gained such an amazing insight into his character? You don't even know him and frankly I must tell you you haven't made much of an impression on him, despite that exotic skin. Or perhaps *because* of it. Hothouse plants like you and Marianne would die out here in the glaring sun.'

Nicole collapsed gracefully into a chair, holding up a restraining hand. 'You've made your point. Just why, I don't know. I have a deep affection for Christine and now Helen, and I'm grateful to Quinn for allowing me to come here, but I find no man worth the pain of loving.'

Margot stared down at her, frowning and concentrating. 'I'm sorry, I've upset you?'

'Not as badly as all that!' Nicole shook back her thick, gleaming hair. 'I'm here for a holiday, that's all, and I'll make a point of leaving before I'm asked.'

'Yes, I think that's best,' Margot said in a mollified fashion. 'By the way, I'd like to thank you. I realise you're trying to help Wayne all you can. Perhaps it's the beginning of a romance?' She clapped her hands delightedly. 'Now that I think about it, you'd be good for him and you'd make a very handsome couple. Perhaps your father might be able to help him as well. He must have all the right connections?'

Nicole lifted her beautiful, gentle face with an immense

effort. 'Talent promotes itself, Margot. We must wait and see how the portrait turns out.'

'I'm sure it will be lovely.' Margot moved to the door and looked back over her square shoulders. 'You dewy, fragile girls look well in a frame. I don't need any such protection.'

After she had gone Nicole sat quietly in the armchair, trying to calm the inner agitation she had never shown. Margot's visit had upset her, to say the least, but it seemed nothing compared to Quinn's destructive passion. In spite of his discipline, the hard strength in him, he had succumbed if only for a few moments to her woman's beauty. His hunger for her she had felt even if she knew he was strong enough, *ruthless* enough, to reject her. She felt vulnerable and very afraid, for though his lovemaking had brought her no peace it had released her from her lonely prison. It even seemed to her that she couldn't recall Peter's face, or his betraying vindictiveness when she told him there wasn't going to be a wedding after all. Youth and inexperience had led her to a broken engagement and long months of despair. Surely after weathering one storm with so much devotion and help she couldn't lay herself open to a far more bitter experience. Because of Quinn and his obliterating aura, Peter was only a shadow now. She could thank him for it, only she discovered he had already hurt her enormously.

CHAPTER SIX

The following week gave Nicole a breathing space, for Quinn flew Margot and Wayne back to Willunga before flying to the State capital to attend a cattlemen's conference. As State President he had to be there and it was no secret that he had a great deal to say. Nicole had often listened with interest to the menfolk's conversations and she was beginning to feel very strongly for the case Quinn was expected to present. Though the Rossiter clan had many other financial interests, including mineral exploration, it was for and on behalf of a big major industry that Quinn worked most tirelessly. Sapphire was an historic station and cattle had first won the Rossiters their fortune.

Without him the days lacked their peculiarly exciting flavour, but there was still beauty and peace and a lot of fun. Kim very smartly informed Nicole that it was *his* turn now, so sometimes, with Christine to make up a threesome, he took her all over the property explaining day-to-day operations, including her in smokos, laughing at her first attempt to return a breakaway steer, and altogether imbuing her further with a deep, satisfying love for outback life. Mostly, tired out but happy after a whole day on the go, they sat out on the veranda for an hour or so after dinner, talking lazily and listening to Paddy's atrocious pop records, that floated so painfully clear on the night air.

It was Christine who suggested they should fly over one day and see Rosalind and her family, and later as they washed up the supper plates she told Nicole why, her pretty face flushing, and her blue eyes earnest.

'Kim's a little annoyed with me,' she said wryly. 'I suppose I did sound as though I was deliberately arranging things.'

'And weren't you?' Nicole asked lightly, the sparkle of mischief in her dark eyes. 'What's bothering you, Chris? I know you so well.'

'Listen, darling, it's not *you*!' Christine turned to her so swiftly, she almost dropped a cup. 'You're a very beautiful girl, you can't help attracting poor gawking males. Not that Kim's one, but I've been looking and listening, and it's obvious you turn him on.'

'*No!*' Nicole said quickly. 'No, I mean it!'

'I know you do,' Christine assured her, 'but you're a little simple about some things. I used to see you at uni. All the guys used to watch and to wait for you to go by and you never even saw them. You never even saw them when they all tried again. I never have been able to work it out. I wouldn't miss anyone giving *me* the eye!'

'Kim's only being kind to me!' Nicole said so appealingly that it further increased Christine's discomfort.

'You clown!' she said, and went quickly on washing up. 'There's a considerable difference between being kind and lighting up every time he looks your way.'

'I'm sorry!' said Nicole as though she didn't know what to do next.

'It's not your fault!' Christine stood the flowered cake plate on the stand, 'and you've a perfect right to tell me to mind my own business, the thing is I love both of you. I'm fond of Roz too. In fact you might say we all entirely approve of her for Kim.'

'So you feel bound to bring Kim's attraction to me to my notice?'

'It's not a comfortable position to be in,' Christine said apologetically. 'If you cared for Kim or could come to care for him it would immediately change the whole matter, but you just see him as your friend, don't you?'

'You know I do!' Nicole was still standing drying the same plate.

Christine took it from her and instead of putting it down on the table, washed it again. 'I guess I shouldn't have mentioned it at all,' she said with such control Nicole knew she was upset.

'No, I'm glad you did,' Nicole returned honestly. 'I have to believe you. I've seen no sign of it myself. Kim and I have had fun—all three of us have. What does Aunt Helen think?'

'She's just a little perturbed too, sweetie!'

'Perhaps I'd better go home.'

'Oh, Nicky!' Christine spun about swiftly and began to cry. 'You know I don't mean that. We love having you here. I want you to stay here for ever!'

'You can't cry in the dishwater!' Nicole laughed shakily.

'Of course I can!' Christine took hold of herself. 'It's interesting and it sometimes follows a good long talk. I know you were a very bright student and I know you're as good as you're beautiful, I just felt I had to warn you what was happening to Kim, seeing that you didn't see it yourself.'

'I haven't encouraged him in the least. You've all got such lovely easy manners I just thought he was being naturally gallant,' said Nicole, still somewhat perturbed.

Christine drew off her soapy gloves and dried her hands. 'He's charming, I grant you, but he's not always so intense about it. He saw through my little plan, of course, and was naturally annoyed by it, but when he sees Roz again he might get his infatuation for you in hand.'

'Do you really believe it?' Nicole asked, and gazed unseeingly outside the window.

'No doubt at all, sweetie,' Christine said briskly. 'And no need to worry your head about it. In a way it's a shame you can't care for him, I'd like you in the family for ever. Poor little Roz now, it would tear her up. She's loved Kim for years. She's a nice girl, you'll like her.'

'Wouldn't it be better if I stayed home?' Nicole asked, leaning forward to hang up the tea-towel.

'No, don't do that!' Christine said seriously. 'Kim might refuse to go. Who knows, I might be in trouble already. He'd be very angry if he thought I was interfering in his life.'

'Well, there's that!' said Nicole, and had to smile. 'It's never simple to take sides in love affairs.'

'I just don't want him to get hurt needlessly. I know what hell you've been through and I don't want Kim to upset you either. Forewarned is forearmed, so they say.'

'No doubt I could introduce a missing lover,' Nicole said a little unhappily, 'but I don't think I will. Actually I don't want to have anything to do with love at all.'

'I doubt whether you could avoid it however hard you tried. You've just got something, that's all—a distinctive allure all your own. As Quinn said so prophetically, you're the sort of woman men fight over.'

Nicole saw him saying it and something touched her, pierced her with pain. 'I think Quinn can be cruel when he likes.' In the strong overhead light her facial bones had a pure, delicate strength, but there was a hurt look in her large dark eyes. 'Never tell him about Peter.'

'Nicky!' Christine put her arm around her anxiously. 'Forget Peter and look towards tomorrow. It's been our great pleasure, Mother's and mine, to see you looking so much happier. You're getting back all your old glow. Peter always drove like a maniac, you know. Maybe not with you, he was always on his best behaviour, but others have told me he gloried in owning a fast car!'

Nicole couldn't speak and Christine leaned sideways and kissed her on the cheek. 'Let's go back to Mamma. She'll be wondering what's kept us so long. Forgive me, Nicky, for speaking?'

'There's nothing to forgive,' Nicole said simply. 'It's all right, really, Chris,' she added gently.

'That's my girl! If you must know,' Christine whispered confidingly as she switched off the light, 'I want you for Quinn!'

By the time they reached Helen's sitting room Nicole was shaking inside, though she managed to smile and act with her usual poise. Helen looked up calmly from her needlework and smiled at them. 'Kim went down to have a word with Paddy. Poor Paddy! He doesn't seem to realise he's doing damage to his eardrums, let alone ours.' Her indulgent expression didn't change as she glanced at both girls. 'What have you planned on tomorrow?'

Christine took a deep breath and plunged into an explanation. 'I asked Kim if he'd take us over to Radcliffe. I'd like Nick to meet Roz and the family.'

Helen's sea blue eyes fixed themselves intently on her daughter's face. 'Now then, Chris, what is this all about?'

Christine shook her head slightly, suddenly detesting herself. 'Machinations, darling!' she said in a tone of regret. 'You know, cooking something up.'

'So that's what was wrong with Kim. He seemed quite put out.' Helen pressed her lips together and looked down at her silks. 'You're such a sensible girl, usually.'

Nicole waited for Christine to speak, then when she didn't she sank down by Helen's side. 'Do you believe Kim is attracted to me, Aunt Helen?' she asked gently.

'My dear child, we all are!' Helen said warmly. 'But I must answer you in the way that you mean. Yes, dear, you're a very beautiful young girl and Kim is romantic and very susceptible to such unusual charm of manner. I take it, from my daughter's face, you've had a little discussion.'

'I didn't see it at all!' Nicole said rather helplessly. 'I like Kim so much I don't want to talk about him in this way.'

'Especially as he may return at any minute!' Helen added dryly. 'My heart aches for all you young things, but I'm a great believer in letting you all work it out for yourselves. At this stage I really can't say who's going to marry who. Certainly Rosalind and Kim have always been linked together—not that Kim will thank you, Chris, for interfering in a matter he feels doesn't concern you!'

'I'll go and poison myself!' Christine said despairingly.

'Don't be silly, dear—besides, you meant well. What concerns me most is, you might have upset Nicole.'

Nicole started a little and colour came into her face. 'I hope Chris and I can talk about anything, Aunt Helen. You've both been so good to me. Knowing what you've told me will help. But really,' she lifted her beautiful dark eyes, 'if you love someone, really *love* them, could you be so susceptible to somebody else?'

Helen stared back at her intently. 'You mean the trouble is more from within than without? It could be. Perhaps not at the end, but in the beginning physical attraction can be very powerful—perhaps the most powerful force in the world. Lots of people never experience anything shattering, others know a genuine passion that lasts all their lives. *I* think it important to share the same background and be good friends and I know such marriages work, but nothing can be harder to fight than an unforgettable face, even when it's gone. Your face, my dear, could haunt a man. I know. I don't know at all about Kim and Roz any more than I know about Quinn and Margot. Both alliances seem very suitable. If either of you think it will help, invite Roz over for the weekend. Kim is rather wound up, but thank God Quinn will be back Friday evening.'

When he did return, reasonably well pleased with the results of the conference, Quinn brought the mail, including a letter from Valerie. Valerie faithfully wrote to her mother each week and Helen looked forward anxiously to these letters as Valerie was going through the last months of her first pregnancy and not feeling very well for most of the time. Over dinner that evening, because Helen was looking particularly concerned, Quinn suggested she fly over to New Zealand for a visit.

'It will set your mind at rest and cheer Val up at the same time.'

Christine nodded agreement and a little glow came into Helen's eyes. 'I don't feel I can leave you, dear. The household must run smoothly. You have so much to do. I take my responsibilities seriously.'

'Don't be silly, Helen!' Quinn glanced at her and gave his rare, beautiful smile. 'At a time like this Val naturally wants her mother. I read the letter. Rob would be pleased to have you too. He must be worrying about Val from the sounds of it. Go over and satisfy yourself everything is all right. The girls can run the household between them. Isn't that right?' He paused and raised his eyebrows and Christine said staunchly:

'Of course we can!'

'Nicole?' He let his glance linger on her for perhaps the first time that night.

'I'll do whatever you want,' she said gravely, lost in the blue brilliance of his eyes.

Helen was clasping and unclasping her small, pretty hands. 'If you think you could manage? The staff have to be supervised. Mary likes me to settle all the menus a week ahead and then there's the paper work, the correspondence to keep up. People might drop in—clients, friends, relatives. They've always done that.' Her fair, youthful face was slightly flushed and uncertain.

'If that's all, Aunt Helen,' Nicole said smilingly, 'Chris and I will take care of it. Mary and I are good friends and I can handle that part of it, if you like. Think how happy Valerie will be to see you!'

Helen smiled radiantly. 'She was such a beautiful bride, Nicky, you've seen the photos.'

'I thought she was very like you. In fact all of your faces are startlingly alike.'

Helen flashed loving eyes towards her stepson. 'Yes, Quinn is the only one to take after my dear Carl. He was such a striking man.'

Kim smiled at Nicole and shook his head slightly. 'Quinn isn't like the rest of us. We're all afflicted by hero-worship, but just don't make the mistake of preferring him to me.'

Quinn's indulgent expression didn't change. 'Do you think it fair to put her on the spot?'

'Really I can answer,' Nicole didn't hesitate. 'I'm not up to heroes. It's quite impossible to meet them on common ground.'

Quinn gave a mocking laugh in his throat, but Kim burst out in delighted astonishment. 'As it stands, brother, that's the first time you've ever been knocked back!'

'And it seems to me Nicole's enjoying it too much!' His black eyebrows arched and Nicole could have smacked his handsome dark face with pleasure. She had indeed enjoyed her little thrust, but now she was blushing.

Christine, seeing the colour in her friend's cheeks, drew the conversation back to the proposed trip to see Valerie and for the rest of the meal Nicole sat quietly while the family worked out the details.

Much later she was standing by herself on the veranda when Kim caught hold of her hand and pulled her down the stairs. 'Let's go for a walk in the moonlight.'

'But I haven't said anything!'

'We won't go far if that's what you're afraid of.'

'Idiot, I feel perfectly safe with you.'

'Then you shouldn't!' He turned to smile at her and his eyes gleamed in the radiant moonlight. 'It's been great having you here, Nicole. I've enjoyed this last week enormously, showing you around, and you haven't seen anything yet. I'd like to take you up in the Piper and fly over the Wild Heart. The view from the air is fantastic, so uniquely Australian. It's not anywhere near as empty and barren as people think. The sand dunes are magnificent, surging across the desert for all the world like the giant waves of the Inland Sea of pre-history, and when the wildflowers are out there just couldn't be a more splendid sight!'

'Not even Sapphire, after rain?' she teased him gently.

'You love it here, don't you?'

'Yes, I do!' She didn't even have to consider. 'All great stations have a certain mystique—the immensity of them and their colourful history. In terms of achievement, the pioneering families deserve nation-wide recognition. It's all so romantic! A colonial mansion set down in the middle of the vast empty plains, the way we all dress for dinner, and the entertaining on the vast scale for the picnic races and the gala balls after the sales. No wonder Sapphire is tagged the Showplace of the South-West. It's more than a small town—and I still haven't met everybody.'

'When the work load slackens we'll be able to show you more,' he told her. 'It's dawn until dusk until the

Wet sets in. Not just the cattle, the dipping, drafting, testing, trucking, but the maintenance of the property, water and power, the aircraft and machinery, the graded roads, and the hundred and one things that need fixing. Of course we've got full-time staff for everything from the saddlemaker to the station store, but you won't find any of us sitting around idle.'

'Certainly not. It all seems very back-breaking to me, but somehow madly enjoyable. I've led such a sheltered life in a way I find station life quite exciting. I suppose the fact that I love horses has a lot to do with it.'

'I've never seen a girl ride better!' Kim paused to look down at her. 'Quinn told me you were fearless to the point of recklessness and I wasn't to allow you to take any chances. Thank you for not giving me anything to worry about.'

'Well, you didn't directly challenge me.'

'And Quinn does?'

'Of course not!' Nicole lifted her head to assure him, her dark hair flowing backwards from the creamy pallor of her skin. 'I simply made him lose his temper.'

'Another first!' Kim said wryly. 'My brother's a man of admirable control and he uses his power lightly—very real power in this part of the world. When Quinn gives an order all of us jump automatically. It has as much to do with presence as actual position. He has the same impact wherever he goes, not just Sapphire. No one could be fairer, all the same I wouldn't suggest you do anything to put yourself on the wrong side of him. My father was killed in a riding accident, did you know?'

'Oh, no!' Nicole gave a faint cry of distress. Christine had never told her how her father died and she had never liked to ask.

'Yes,' Kim replied quietly. 'It was the worst day of our lives. You can't imagine how frightful!'

'I think I can.' Nicole took Kim's hand again and for a moment they walked on through the night with the gardens and parkland bathed in a luminous light. In the distance came the sound of music from one of the staff bungalows; not Paddy's frenetic variety, but dreamy, orchestrated love songs. Nicole listened with a little catch of the heart. One of them had been a favourite of Peter's just as it seemed to be a favourite of Jeb Martin's, the young station accountant, whose girl-friend was a governess on a property five hundred miles away.

Kim, too, appeared to be listening, then he picked up his story. 'The horse that threw Dad was an impossible animal to handle, but Dad didn't like having his ability and authority questioned. He was a superb horseman and he was used to everyone and everything being very respectful. Quinn had ridden Wildfire and that seemed to drive Dad to do the same. Much as he revelled in having Quinn for a son and his heir Dad had a liking for coming out on top. He didn't want Quinn to beat him at anything, even while he was as proud of him as the devil. He was all stirred up the day he took Wildfire out. None of us could have stopped him except Quinn, and he was in Adelaide on business. By the time he got back, Dad was hours dead. Afterwards Quinn disappeared for three days with a rifle. The mare got away to the range. We never knew whether he shot her or let her go, and it will be years before I ask him if I ever do. Dad and Quinn had a very special relationship. I guess he misses him the most.'

'And he never speaks of his mother?' Nicole asked without curiosity but a certain deep melancholy.

'Never!' Kim said abruptly. 'Neither did Dad. That might leave you thinking Marianne was the forgotten woman, but neither of them forgot her, I'm sure of that.'

'Is she still alive?' Nicole asked with the same gravity.

'No,' Kim said in a strange voice. 'She left Quinn a small fortune, but he gave it all away as if it was going to burn him—medical research mostly, and one or two charities. She sent for him at the end, and he went, but he never did speak about it. Quinn just naturally keeps things to himself. Of course he had to be self-sufficient at a very early age.'

Nicole was standing absolutely immobile looking out over the silver and ebony landscape. 'Thank you for telling me, Kim,' she said quietly.

'Maybe it will help you understand a few things.' Kim fixed his eyes on her pure profile. 'My brother is a very strong character, but he was hurt profoundly as a child. When you realise that it accounts for his severe attitude towards women. I don't mean the way he treats them, he can be as charming as hell, and God knows he's anything but neglected, but his bitter disappointment in his mother went very deep. Margot is the only one who's ever stayed the distance. He seems to trust her and she really cares about him. Even so, she can't manipulate him into marriage.'

'I don't know that any woman could do that!' Nicole said with a rare tartness. 'I wouldn't like to be the woman Quinn settles on. You couldn't cling to him or try pushing him away. I think he could make a woman very unhappy, despite all that dark splendour.'

'Not Margot!' Kim laughed beneath his breath. '*She's* not wasting away, and she's not overly sensitive. But I see what you mean, a sweet little thing would just droop in the blaze!' He put out his hands and rested them on Nicole's bare shoulders, looking down into her eyes. 'Have you ever been in love, Nicole?'

A slight tremor went through her body but her dark eyes were sad and calm. 'I thought I was, once. It didn't work out.'

'A man would be a fool to let *you* go!' Kim said intensely. 'Surely you don't still care about him?'

Nicole drew in her breath, conscious of the tenderness in Kim's expression, the way his hands held her shoulders with a yearning pleasure. All that mattered was that she didn't hurt him. She liked him so much, yet she knew beyond doubt she could never care for him in the way he seemed to want. And then there was Rosalind. While he stood staring down at her faintly quizzically it seemed necessary to lie or at least to mislead him.

'Please, Kim,' she said, and started to turn her head away, 'I don't want to talk about it!'

'You don't know me, then.' She heard him reply with a kind of dogged determination. 'I hate to see you unhappy. You're so beautiful!' He picked her up easily like a bold buccaneer, striding back across the grass towards the bright lights of the house.

'Kim!' She began to laugh helplessly and after a minute his momentary violence gave way to a wry humour.

'If you think I'd like to run off with you, you're dead right!'

Too late she saw Quinn standing on the veranda in conversation with Ed Calvin, his head stockman. Both men turned and looked their way and Nicole whispered breathlessly, 'Put me down, Kim!'

But Kim was still laughing, totally unperturbed. He walked up the short flight of stairs before he set her down gently. 'Here's a featherweight for you!' he announced serenely.

'Good evening, Miss Lindfield,' Ed said pleasantly.

Nicole smiled at him, conscious that the shoestring strap of her silk crêpe-de-chine dress had slipped off her shoulder and wisps of her windblown hair were clinging to her flushed cheeks. 'How's Sally going at school?'

'Fine, ma'am, just fine!' Ed looked at Quinn, then back at Nicole. 'I've just given the Boss here his monthly report. Seeing how we all owe him so much Sally likes to tell him exactly how she's doin'. Seems she gained a distinction in a national Maths competition.'

'That's marvellous,' Nicole congratulated him warmly. 'You and Mrs Calvin must be very proud.'

'That we are!' Ed retorted. 'I'll cut along now, Boss. Thanks for everything!' He ran on down the stairs and paused at the bottom, a spare man with a perceptible air of health and good humour. 'Exactly where did you put Mick's new saddle, Kim?'

The question took Kim unawares. 'Didn't I tell Paddy to take care of it?'

'Actually you didn't!'

'Better go find it!' Quinn glanced at his brother. 'He's got to have it in the morning.'

'Right!' Kim moved down the stairs to join Ed. 'Why don't we take the girls out in the morning? Nicky will make a good little camp drafter with practice!'

Much to Nicole's surprise Ed added his agreement. 'It's a treat to see her on a horse, and I've got a good compact little gelding for you to ride, miss.'

Quinn shrugged his wide shoulders. 'We'll see. If we take her someone will have to keep an eye on her all the time.'

'I dunno,' Ed declared, and aimed a swipe at a persistent insect. 'I never expected a city lady to be so smart on a horse. Thanks to Kim, here, she's learned a lot.'

'That's right,' Kim nodded, his blue eyes shining with excitement.

'I'll think about it,' was all Quinn would say.

Ed touched his forehead in a simple salute and both men disappeared around the side of the house, obviously making towards the stables complex.

Nicole had smoothed back her hair and adjusted the thin strap of her dress. Something in Quinn's demeanour was making her feel a faint agitation.

'I'll go inside,' she murmured swiftly, as though eager to escape.

'Not so fast!' As she slipped past him he caught her arm and spun her effortlessly into a chair. 'If you go on like this, you're going to have Kim all confused.'

'That's not my intention!' she said tersely, and linked her trembling fingers.

'I'm sorry, but I don't see it that way.' His hard, handsome mouth curved with contempt. 'Was it really that hard to walk back to the house?'

'You know very well I had nothing to do with that!' She tried to lift herself out of the chair, but he moved swiftly and blocked her, the warmth of his hand searing the violet silk of her dress.

'What is it you want?' he asked with soft menace. 'In some ways Kim's led a very narrow life. It shouldn't be necessary for me to tell you.'

'So what's your worry?' she asked, her temper flaring. There was an angry sparkle in her eyes and at the base of her throat a pulse began a sudden, indignant beating. For the first time in her life she wanted desperately to hurt someone, and that someone was Quinn Rossiter.

'You're all woman. You *know*!' he said tightly. 'After all, you have an ex-fiancé back in the city, probably an everlasting string of admirers. Wayne won't feel happy or fulfilled until he's back here committing magnolia skin and black eyes to canvas. I bet your father has indulged you endlessly, refusing you nothing. I could go on and on. You're beautiful and you look very expensive. I know Kim's never met anyone like you in his life.'

'Aren't you forgetting he's a grown man?' Nicole said

turbulently, holding her voice down with a great effort. 'He's free to pick his own friends.'

'We're not talking about *friends*!' he returned flatly. 'Probably this is only a pleasant diversion for you, but I don't want him hurt.'

Nicole clenched her slender hands so they wouldn't fly out and hit him. 'You're all heart!' she said bitterly, the furious tears rushing into her eyes. 'And you're overlooking something important. Kim's not like you, with your heart in a prison. He hasn't sacrificed all emotion or given it up as a weakness. He's not afraid to feel. You talk as if I'm trying to exploit him, exploit every man I meet. It's so ridiculous, and it couldn't be further from the truth!'

'Fancy that!' His upraised hand silenced her instantly. 'We're to take it you're truly an unwilling femme fatale?'

His voice had a cutting, inflexible quality that had her swinging up excitedly out of the high-backed peacock chair. 'Oh, *shut up*!' she said wretchedly. 'You've had a down on me from the first moment we met.'

'And I thought I was covering it rather well!' His voice was metallic, unbearably cynical. 'Be warned, little one!'

She gave a sad, scornful laugh and blinked her eyelashes rapidly. 'If you've finished upsetting me I'm going inside.'

'Stay here for a moment!' His tone was cool and commanding. 'I want you to promise me you won't give Kim any more encouragement.'

Nicole gave a short laugh and went to walk past him, but his hands gripped her shoulders, holding her in front of him. 'I want you to promise me *now*!'

'You won't listen, will you?' It was no use. Her voice broke. She stood there, her head bent, fighting the terrifying urge to just lean against him, to have him hold her, even in violence. She could never reach him and he could only resent her.

'Nicole?'

She shut her eyes quickly, fighting for composure. 'Please, Quinn, *please*!' she implored.

'Do you think I blame a man for desiring you?' he asked with intensity. 'I'm trying to protect you as well. You're such a little fool, perhaps you can't help it.' He pushed his hand through her hair and tilted her head back. 'Some women only bring anguish, and you're one of them. I understand that.'

'Then why don't you send me away?' Almost against her will she moved closer to him and his hands tightened on her even while his blue eyes were blazing.

'I'd like to hold you until you were crying in my arms!'

A tear dashed against her cheek and he released her abruptly, but with ruthless purpose. 'When you go inside Chris will tell you that she's been on to Radcliffe. Personally I think that's wise. Roz is a nice girl and she's best qualified to make Kim happy. He used to think so himself before you arrived!'

'Why don't you set yourself up as a marriage broker?' she asked tauntingly, but not before she had reached the safety of the hallway. 'A pity you're scared of it yourself!'

Unexpectedly Quinn gave a hoot of laughter, his jewelled glance sliding over her until she was quivering with anger. 'Only with a little witch like you!' he returned cuttingly. 'It would be so foolish, wouldn't it, Nicole? Some men are easily duped by a woman's beauty, but not me. I learned early though it hurt at the time.'

Nicole turned away quickly, her heart beating so fast she might have run up a hundred stairs. It was a mistake to try to goad him, for he had a cruel streak. Let Margot court the devil! She was welcome to a lifetime of woe and maybe brief moments of glittering excitement. She was no seeker of danger herself, however thrilling.

A minute later Christine appeared along the gallery, leaning over and calling to her friend. 'Where on earth have you been? We want you to help decide on Mamma's wardrobe for New Zealand.'

'I'll come right away!' Gratefully Nicole flew up the stairway, secure in the knowledge that at least Helen and Christine regarded her with uncomplicated affection.

CHAPTER SEVEN

HELEN had only been gone a few days when the first of a chain of minor mishaps occurred. Mela, one of the little aboriginal housegirls, brought down a Japanese temple vase on herself while she was dusting and in rushing to see what her charge had done next, Mary missed her footing coming down the stairs and suffered the shock of a fall and a sprained ankle.

Nicole found her white-faced and moaning at the base of the stairs with Mela clutching a beautiful broken piece of porcelain in her bleeding hand and wailing as if Mary was about to depart the earth for the sky people.

'Stop that, Mela!' Nicole said so firmly Mela immediately turned off her remarkable show of desolation. 'Have you hurt yourself badly? Show me!' While she spoke Nicole put her arm around Mary's shoulders both of them gazing with dismay at Mary's quickly swelling ankle.

Mela thrust her hand under Nicole's nose, her nerve clearly shattered, and after a glance to satisfy herself the cut was superficial Nicole told her to go and wash it in the first aid room, use some disinfectant, wrap something around it and go find Miss Christine who had gone down to the office building.

'What a stupid thing to happen!' Mary upbraided herself. 'I've been coming down these stairs for the best part of twenty years!' Sweat had broken out over her temples and around her mouth and she had gone very white.

'Don't talk, Mary, you've had a shock.' Nicole looked down at her anxiously. 'I think I'll remove your shoe

before the ankle swells any more, then we must get someone to move you.'

Mela at that moment burst back into the hallway with
her hand swathed in a clean bandage. 'Goin' right away,
miss!' she cried urgently.

Nicole just nodded and while Mary set her teeth she
gently unlaced Mary's comfortable flat shoe and drew
it carefully off her injured foot. 'I'd say that was a bad
sprain!' she commented, and lifted her eyes to Mary's
pleasant, kindly face. 'How do you feel?'

'A bit shaken!' Mary said ruefully. 'That little tinker,
Mela, not that I can blame her for my falling down the
stairs. That vase, you know, was one of Mrs Rossiter's
favourites. I've told Mela plainly she's not to dust any
of those things.'

Mela, at least, went like the wind, for within a few
minutes Christine was back with Jeb Martin and Les
Taylor, the station vet. Though she laughed about it,
Mary let Les examine her ankle and later both men
linked hands to carry her to the quiet comfort of her
room.

It meant that temporarily they were without a housekeeper and Chester, the cook for the station hands, was
without Mary's invaluable aid in whipping up piles of
pikelets and scones for the morning and afternoon
smokos. Mary herself seemed so upset the girls told her
without hesitation that between them they could manage
until Mary was on her feet again. After all, as Christine
reasoned, she had to learn to cook some time.

Her first effort sat making scones was so disastrous
there was no use even sending them down to the men.
Christine settled herself on the edge of the table and
watched Nicole frantically whipping up batch upon batch
of crunchy little butter biscuits flavoured with anything
she could put her hands on readily; raw peanuts and

spices, walnuts and hazel nuts and the last batch, because
Christine wasn't watching, burnt butter.

Afterwards they found out these little offerings had
gone down very well with the men, but next morning
when Quinn found Nicole turning dough over in the
kitchen at five-thirty he took a different view of her
efforts. He had come in so silently she almost sprang
away from the table in fright.

'What the devil are you doing?' he exclaimed.

He was so obviously surprised to see her there, she
laughed. 'Making hot baps for breakfast. They'll be ready
in just a little over ten minutes.' She turned away from
him to check on the sausages she had set to cook very
slowly. The range was enormous and there was plenty of
room to cook the eggs in any way they wanted as well
as the tomatoes and bacon. Nicole's own appetite had
sharpened remarkably in the past weeks and she expected to enjoy her own efforts.

'You don't have to do that!' he said so curtly she
swung around to face him.

'But I *want* to! Besides, Mary would have no peace
at all if she thought one of us wasn't getting your breakfast.'

'Damn it, we can get it ourselves!'

'Are you usually such a sorehead first thing in the
morning?' Nicole asked as if she knew. She felt dangerously close to happiness—but happiness couldn't lie
with this uncompromisingly hard and handsome man.

He was silent so long she looked up at him only to find
him watching her with the most curious expression.
'What is it?' The slanting rays of the sun revealed her
flawless morning face, dark eyes clear and faintly bewildered.

'I don't know if I like a strange woman in my kitchen.'
His mouth curved in a smile, but there was no trace of
amusement in his eyes.

'I thought you told me I was no stranger?' she returned a little sombrely.

He walked past her and lifted the tea and coffee canisters down from the shelf. 'Don't remember *too* much, Nicole!'

'Maybe I can't help myself!' She hadn't meant to say it, but somehow it came out.

Quinn turned around to face her and she was more than ever aware of his stunning physical fitness and health. A button was hanging loosely on his blue denim shirt and instinctively she put out a hand to check whether it was about to fall off or not.

'Don't worry about it!' He caught her fingers and twisted them in his own.

'You'll loosen it!'

'I have dozens of shirts.'

She turned her head a little dizzily, fighting off the blue shock of his gaze. 'There's plenty to do, Quinn, you'd better let me go.' He seemed to be towering over her, his very proximity making the blood rush to her head.

'All right,' his voice was faintly mocking, 'you're here, so now we'll see what you can do.'

'I'll have you know we cooked dinner last night—or didn't that register?' she asked pertly.

'*You* cooked dinner, magnolia, my little sister is incapable of boiling an egg.'

Though this seemed true enough Nicole hastened to Christine's defence. 'When you've been used to a housekeeper all your life. . . .'

'What about you?' He caught her arm as she crossed briskly to and fro.

'Excuse me!' she prompted gently.

'I'll let you go when you tell me.'

'Very well—my mother died when I was a small child but my dear Aunt Sarah made it her business to see I became thoroughly domesticated. I know you think I'm hideously incapable, but I really enjoy running our home for my father. He's a very busy man and very pressured for most of the time, so the house must run smoothly. I'm a good cook and I'm a good hostess, thanks to Aunt Sarah.'

'And who's looking after your father now?' He gave her an intent look that made her return it.

'Aunt Sarah, of course, with a little household help.'

Kim, hearing voices in the kitchen, burst in with a look of surprise that quickly turned to pleasure and satisfaction. 'Say, are you going to have breakfast with us, Nicky?'

'I'm going to cook it if you'll let me!' Cheeks flushed, Nicole popped the baps in the oven. 'Which way do you like your eggs?'

For answer Kim crossed the kitchen in a few giant strides and gave her a little hug. 'Honestly, this is fantastic!'

'I'm sure it is,' Quinn murmured dryly, 'so we'll leave Nicole absolutely on her own for the next ten minutes. Come on—down to the office!'

Kim followed his brother to the door still smiling. 'It's all a bit overwhelming, Nicky. Is there anything you can't do?'

'She couldn't live her entire life on the desert fringe,' said Quinn as though he was sure in his own mind.

Kim looked a little uncomfortable, then his high spirits revived. 'Well, at least she's enjoying it now, and so am I! By the way, sweet, we like our eggs fried with lots of bacon and maybe a couple of those sausages. Tea for me, black coffee for Quinn, hot and strong. Throw in a little juice and some cereal and that will be perfect.'

Nicole glanced up at the wall clock and smiled. 'Breakfast will be ready in *exactly* fifteen minutes!'

An hour later Nicole took breakfast on a tray to Mary

and stayed chatting over her third cup of tea. Mary's white, sick look had quite disappeared, but it was obvious she wouldn't be up and about for the best part of a week. That morning, however, Nicole quite conquered Mary's little fears and anxieties, assuring her there was no need to worry and the little enforced rest would do her the world of good. It was further decided that from a comfortable chair in the shade, Mary could direct a couple of houseboys in the extension of the already huge kitchen gardens.

When Christine sauntered downstairs a little after eight she found Nicole in the sunroom writing a long letter home. 'Hi, pal!' Christine said, and smiled. 'What time did you get up?'

'About five.' Nicole turned her writing pad over and put down her pen.

'You didn't!' Christine rubbed her tiptilted nose.

'Actually I got breakfast for the men.'

'How perfectly splendid!' Christine collapsed into a chair. 'I'm sure Quinn was cross with you. This is supposed to be your holiday!'

'And so it is, darling. I was just telling Father and Aunt Sarah how good it's been for me out here.'

'I'm glad!' Christine leant over and patted her friend's hand. 'You're an awfully nice person, Nicky. You've got lots of character.'

'You're just saying that because you know I've got your breakfast ready,' smiled Nicole.

'Have you really!' Christine stretched as though she still wasn't properly awake. 'That's sweet of you, but you're not to bother from now on.'

'It's all right, really,' Nicole looked with deep affection at her friend. 'I like doing these little things—besides, breakfast was a great success. Quinn thanked me very smoothly, but Kim wasn't nearly so reticent!' She stood up with a very sweet smile touching her mouth. 'By the way, what are you going to do about Rosalind?'

'What indeed?' Christine returned rather wryly. 'She's missing Kim terribly, but what with Mamma having to go over to Val so unexpectedly we had to put her stay off. Now Mary's demobilised it sort of makes things impossible.'

'But how?' Nicole had to smile. 'What's one more girl to feed?'

'Aren't you forgetting Wayne's trying to get back as well?'

'We haven't heard anything definite.'

'You will!' Christine said almost gloomily. 'Poor Wayne, I think he's doomed to be a failure.'

'You know, I feel very sorry for him,' Nicole said. 'He keeps comparing himself with Quinn; a man so unlike himself.'

'You can say that again!' Christine spoke wryly.

'It shouldn't matter so much. What Wayne should do is find a more suitable environment. On his own admission he doesn't like station life, yet from what you tell me he's a gifted artist. If he needs the city life to thrive why doesn't he go there? If he can't make the front rank as a painter why doesn't he open a gallery or something? At least he'd be working and living in his own world.'

Christine lifted her head and for the first time Nicole saw there were shadows under her eyes. 'No one's ever suggested that before—about the gallery, I mean. Wayne's so helplessly apathetic. Of course his mother adored him and spoilt him, though she did want him to *try*. The trouble is Wayne's so unlike anyone but himself. Margot's so strong and uncomplicated and all Wayne needs is understanding. I hate it!'

'But you want to like him, don't you?' Nicole asked gently.

'I can't think why!' Christine turned her fair head away to look out the big picture window. 'It's rather unpleasant to care about a man one can't admire.'

'Let me get you your breakfast,' Nicole said soothingly. 'And about Rosalind, why don't you call her this morning? I'm looking forward to meeting her.'

'Oh, you'll like her,' Christine said more cheerfully, 'and she'll like you. But it's really up to Quinn.'

'He won't mind,' Nicole answered rather dryly.

'Don't tell me he's spoken to you——' Christine began, but Nicole held up her hand.

'Breakfast coming up, Miss Rossiter!' Then when Christine went to push up to help her, she waved her down. 'There can't be two cooks in the kitchen!'

'What a relief!' Christine subsided with a grin. 'As a personal favour to your old friend you'll have to give me a few lessons before you go home. Mary has always chased me.'

'Will do!' Nicole glanced back and smiled.

In the end Kim went to fetch Rosalind, and Nicole found herself liking the other girl from the very first moment. Rosalind wasn't quite as attractive as Nicole expected, indeed she was rather shy and kept glancing at Nicole nervously, but when the first little awkwardness wore off, Nicole saw she was possessed of a pretty wit, lovely light grey eyes that went well with her chestnut hair, and a quiet charm of manner. Kim, who rarely fell victim to moods, seemed quite pleased to have her there and in the days that followed Nicole had reason to feel grateful to Rosalind for her assistance. Despite her reassurances to Mary, there was a great deal to do and Nicole began to think she wouldn't have managed nearly so well without Rosalind's unsolicited, unstinting help. Christine liked office work much better and she attended to all the station's correspondence, answering what she could, and leaving the rest to Quinn.

Though she saw him at breakfast and dinner, it seemed to Nicole that Quinn was avoiding her, so it came as a surprise when he told her, not asked her, that he was taking her out in the jeep the next morning. Dinner was over and Rosalind had offered to make the coffee, but Quinn turned away with just the faintest touch of irritation, explaining that he and Kim had work to do.

'Is anything wrong?' Rosalind asked breathlessly, after the men had gone off to Quinn's study. 'Quinn seemed a little cross.'

'It was a long hard day,' Christine explained. 'No wonder he wants to have an hour or so off in the morning.'

'I don't want him to put himself out for me!' Nicole got up and started to load the dishes on to the trolley.

'Let me do that!' Rosalind offered instinctively. 'You got dinner.'

'Oh, for goodness' sake why don't you let the girls do the dishes?' Christine cried.

'You know the answer to that one!' Nicole turned around to finish the job, 'there are lots of jobs I trust to the girls, but plates seem to slide out of their hands.'

'Hmm!' Christine nodded, then laughed. 'The thing is you two make me go limp.' She stood up and began collecting the beautiful long-stemmed crystal wine glasses. 'Wayne called in before dinner, did you know?'

'Really?' Nicole slid her eyes around to look at Christine. 'Who spoke to him?'

'Quinn,' Christine answered unsmilingly.

'He's anxious to get on with Nicole's portrait, of course!' said Rosalind with an admiring glance at Nicole from under her thick golden-brown lashes. 'You're so beautiful, Nicole—but I suppose you've been told that every day since you were a baby?'

Nicole smiled and if there was a little tang of bitterness in her mouth Rosalind didn't notice it. 'I wonder why Quinn didn't mention it, about Wayne,' she spoke directly to Christine who was standing looking down at the table with a preoccupied frown on her face.

'I gather he doesn't want him here.'

'So he told him no?'

'I expect so. He didn't say and just then I didn't care to press him. Paddy and Albert lost a big mob in the scrub today. They just bolted, split up and vanished, according to Paddy. I gather there were fireworks when they rode back. Bert always likes to bustle them and cattle just won't be hurried. They've been told to collect them tomorrow or just keep on going. Quinn likes a clean muster every single time.'

'Well, something's got him stirred up,' Rosalind said artlessly. 'I'll give it a few minutes, then I'll take their coffee along to the study.'

'Thanks, Rosalind.'

'No problem!' Rosalind returned Nicole's smile. 'After all, it's your holiday. You should be relaxing.'

'But I am. You don't know how much.'

Rosalind's eyelids drooped over her large grey eyes. 'It seems silly now, but I was so nervous of meeting you. I somehow thought you'd be quite different—you know, very citified and formal.'

'What nonsense, Roz!' Christine spoke a little briskly. 'After all, Nicky is my friend. That sort of person wouldn't appeal to me at all. As you can see, she's really a homebody and she loves the rural life.'

'Yes, it was the greatest possible relief to find you so natural.' Rosalind smiled at Nicole apologetically. 'And you're really kind. I hope you have the happiest possible stay.'

And more than anything you don't want me to take Kim away from you, Nicole thought compassionately, detecting the faint cloud in Rosalind's grey eyes. Though there was no malice at all in Rosalind's quiet nature Nicole was aware that the other girl had been somewhat surprised to find Nicole wasn't one of the spoilt, pampered darlings of this world. She wished she could have comforted her a lot more about Kim, but Kim's eyes and manner were a dead give-away to the pleasure he took in Nicole's company. Understandably this pained Rosalind and tactfully Nicole tried to avoid drawing Kim's attention and interest, but it was by no means simple. Kim, as they had all come to know, was a very determined young man and he too was accustomed to getting his own way.

The birds always woke her. Nicole lifted the mosquito net and went to the window. It was a beautiful morning, cool yet scented, the pre-dawn silence shattered by the clamour of the birds. They streaked from tree to tree in flashes of exotica; a dazzling display of coloured wings, blue, green, pink, yellow and orange; a glowing world of colour and sound. A mad cackle broke out in the limewoods and she lifted her eyes to look for the brown and white plumage of the woodland kingfisher, the kookaburra. She couldn't see it, but its pealing, raucous, building hysterics almost drowned out the rest of the feathered orchestra. The ancients would have defied such a unique bird, she supposed.

Moving swiftly, she washed, then dressed in jeans and a fine pinky beige cotton T-shirt. Excitement was moving in her, running warmly through her veins. God help her, but she was looking forward to this outing like nothing else she had ever known. Quinn wanted to leave early, straight after breakfast before the heat became too intense, and as they were going to take the jeep she picked up a silk bandana and her wide-brimmed natural straw panama.

When she entered the kitchen, Rosalind rounded from

the range with a smile. 'Hi, you look as fresh as the morning!'

'I slept well. And you?'

'Actually it took me an age to drift off.' Briskly Rosalind broke eggs into the flying pan. 'I'm getting breakfast this morning, I hope you don't mind?'

'Not at all. It's very kind of you, Roz. Do you need any help?'

'You could set the table.'

'As good as done!' Nicole returned pleasantly. 'I haven't been fussing. We've just been sitting at the long table instead of the breakfast room. Neither Quinn nor Kim seem to mind.'

Rosalind turned around, a small neat figure in her everyday uniform, jeans and a bright shirt, but there was a shadow in her large grey eyes. 'I suppose they'll be as surprised to see me as you are?'

'Don't you mean *pleased*?' Nicole asked gently and threw a clean cloth over the long Spanish table.

Without make-up and her scattering of golden freckles showing clearly, Rosalind looked little more than a child. 'You know how I feel about Kim, don't you, Nicole? I suppose it shows?'

Nicole decided it would be better to show surprise than admit she had heard all about it. 'I know you're very fond of him, Roz, and he certainly is of you!'

'I love him,' Rosalind declared with quiet passion. 'I can hardly remember a time when I didn't.'

'Well, he's a very fine young man,' Nicole said agreeably, her hands moving with quick precision around the table, placing the cutlery. 'What's important too is that you have a great deal in common.'

'I think I'd much prefer he was madly in love with me!' Rosalind returned so rapidly she almost stuttered. 'I should be beautiful——'

'You look perfectly all right to me,' Nicole insisted.

'You've got lovely colouring and I've always admired grey eyes.'

'But I haven't got quite what it takes!' Ruefully Rosalind turned back to the enormous range, checking on the progress of the eggs and the steak. 'The trouble with me is I've got no mystery, no mystery at all. A woman needs magnetism. Like you.'

It was a direct reference and Nicole took a moment to answer. 'That's great for my morale, Roz, but the fact is beauty or magnetism or whatever you like to call it, is no guarantee of happiness. You have everything you need in your own pretty face and manner. Add to that, you're cheerful, intelligent and very competent, and you should have no difficulty at all in getting your man!'

'If it were only that simple!' Rosalind said between her teeth. 'If I lost Kim I'd feel finished, empty.'

'Why are you presuming you have lost him?' Nicole asked directly.

'Oh, forgive me!' Rosalind put her head in her hands, looking so small and pathetic that Nicole moved towards her and put her arm around her.

'Don't, Roz! Don't upset yourself!'

'I'm so ashamed!' sighed Rosalind.

'Why, for being human? But please don't see me as a threat, Roz.'

'Oh, I don't want to!' Rosalind muttered, looking incredibly young. 'I only know Kim could lose his head very easily over you and the funny part is, I don't blame him in the least!'

It was embarrassing as well as upsetting and Nicole found herself loathing the whole situation. Neither did she know how to cope with this unexpected emotional involvement. How strange it was that she should arouse Kim when her own feelings for him were very much fraternal.

Happily Rosalind dried her tears before the men came
in and though Quinn glanced at her rather sharply he
said nothing but ate in near-silence while Kim, looking
blissfully tanned and carefree, insisted on getting up and
down helping Nicole to more coffee and toast, his blue
eyes against his sun-drenched skin full of a transparent
admiration.

'Would you mind taking pity on us as well?' Quinn
broke in rather tersely.

'Gosh, I'm sorry!' said Kim with a little laugh, and
turned around to Rosalind looking down at her chestnut
curls. 'Could you possibly have some more, Shortie?'

The petite Rosalind, so addressed, to Kim's deep
perplexity suddenly shoved back her chair and raced
from the kitchen.

'I'm worried about that kid!' Kim said to no one.

'Why don't you go after her?' Nicole suggested
quickly. 'You should be able to catch her easily.'

'What for? She could be sick or something.'

'For God's sake!' Quinn pitched away his napkin and
stood up, pushing his hand over his crisp, dark hair. 'You
know the child worships you, yet you've been tormenting
her continually by dancing attendance on Nicole.'

'Excuse me!' Nicole said, and got up quickly herself. 'The last thing *I* want is to be admired by anyone.'
Her thick lashes swept downwards and colour burned in
her cheeks.

'Never mind about Nicole!' Quinn clamped his hand
on his brother's shoulder. 'Go after Roz!'

Kim was still eyeing Nicole, looking worried, and
Quinn nearly spun him to the door. 'You can't possibly
call a woman Shortie when she's dying of love for you. I
insist you apologise.'

'Oh, all right!' Kim pushed himself on his way looking
for all the world as if the whole thing was incomprehen-

sible to him. 'I'll never understand women.'

'Don't try!' Quinn returned sardonically, and Nicole was struck by the cynical look in his brilliant blue eyes.

A few minutes later when they were walking out to the jeep they could see Kim and Rosalind in deep conversation. Rosalind was sitting on the garden wall and Kim was leaning over her with one hand on her shining curls.

'Why the sigh?' Quinn asked Nicole abruptly.

She didn't answer him deliberately, suffering her own torment. Quinn was such a cruel brute. If he hadn't practically pushed her out of the house she wouldn't have consented to go with him at all. Anyone would think she was the eternal temptress craving the thrill of conquest instead of a girl who just wanted to be left alone.

Their route took them past the staff bungalows where children were playing in a special little playground of their own equipped with all manner of adventurous and conventional things, and Nicole returned the ready waves while Quinn lightly touched the horn. It was a relief at least to see his face soften, and though he was very much the Boss with everyone, the children weren't in the least shy of him.

Outside the perimeter of the homestead and its satellite buildings, they went like the wind, speeding across the peaceful flats where the cattle were grazing, through the belt of trees that made green oases in the ochre plains and on towards the flat-topped mesas lapped by a blue sea of mirage at their feet. A group of aboriginal women with a kindergarten of children were on the edge of the Pink Lady Lagoon, a moon-shaped area of lush green and a tea tree-shaded deep billabong where pink waterlilies flowered in great numbers. The sight of them in such a place was as natural and appealing as the great profusion of storm lilies that appeared like magic after the slightest fall of rain, multiplying at an astounding rate and lavishly decorating the flats with pale pink and cream.

'Aren't you even going to ask where we're going?' Quinn asked unexpectedly.

'Sometimes with you I get the feeling silence is golden.'

'Better put your hat on,' he advised her, not even bothering to answer her statement.

Nicole's black hair was blowing back in the breeze like a banner, a wild fall of silk that spun around her face as she turned to him. 'I will in a moment. I'm enjoying this, the breeze is so sweet and fresh like wild honey.'

'You won't enjoy sunburn!' he pointed out rather caustically.

'You *are* in a bad temper,' she observed drily.

'I am not!' Briefly his blue eyes assaulted her face.

'I suppose not!' Obediently she secured her hat beneath her chin. '*That* would have the impact of dynamite.'

'Take care then you don't invite a blast.'

'Maybe I will anyway,' she said wryly, and laughed as an emu ran up from a steep gully and began to pace the racing jeep.

'They're fantastic birds, aren't they?' she added.

'Second only to the ostrich. That fellow must be close to six feet. The tiny wings are hidden in the feathers.' As he was speaking Quinn took his foot off the accelerator until the speedometer fell back to around fifty kilometres an hour. The emu was still running strongly, its long sturdy legs moving effortlessly.

'It's racing us deliberately, isn't it?' asked Nicole.

'It seems to be. In a minute it'll get bored. Sheep men don't usually like emus, they break down the fences. I used to have an emu for a pet when I was a small boy. The damned thing was nearly human. After that I had a kangaroo I raised from a joey of six months old. As an adult male it stood seven feet high and it could leap over any obstacle in the compound. It didn't seem to have the slightest desire to join the mob and it was as faithful and tame as any of our dogs. In fact Digger and the dogs were very friendly. They howled for days after he died.'

'Of what?'

'He had a mate, of course, he used to visit in the bush. Unfortunately he got into a fight with a particularly big and vicious dingo hound called Juluk, a real killer we hunted for years. We found Juluk's body a couple of days later, but poor old Digger bled to death before we could save him. It appeared later that Juluk attacked the female first, but Digger kicked right in to defend her. The female used to come right in with her joey looking for Digger for a long time—which says something for fidelity in the wild.'

'Are we making for that big flat top hill?' she asked with a child's curiosity.

'We are!' he said with a faint smile on his face. 'From there the view is superb—the great empty unknown. In times of drought the tribal elders go there and perform their magic rain dances. I've seen winds come up howling and threshing, the sky filling with silver and purple clouds and still not a drop. The old fellows increase their plenty magic and it sometimes happens that we get a fair sprinkling of rain. As you've seen yourself since you've been on Sapphire, rain has a dramatic effect on the desert plains. Even the barren ridges are covered in wildflowers. From Mokani, that's where we're going, you'll get some idea of the desert beauty without actually flying over it or driving into it. It's the highest point I can take you and we'll have to climb. There are much higher flat tops, but they'd be too difficult for you.'

'I'm not a grandmother!' she exclaimed with a slight expression of indignation.

'My dear girl, *my* grandmother could have walked you off your legs.'

'Grandmother Rossiter, you mean?'

'I think you know that very well!' he returned crisply. 'My other grandmother, I understand, was a little butterfly creature.'

Nicole turned her head from his remote profile. Under the brim of his hat it was strong and perfect, but hard. Without seeing the brilliant shock of colour of his eyes he was as dark as an Indian, and like an Indian his skin was polished more than weathered. He was a very handsome man, but he was too tough to soften, too unyielding to move. Such men could really defeat a woman. Nicole fell silent while the warm, scented wind blew stronger, lifting the fragrance of the earth into the air like blue silk.

As they approached Mokani they rolled in and out of sandy troughs covered in grey-green cushions of spinifex, a myriad of them, round and spiky. A huge lizard shot out from behind one clump, but Nicole had yet to see her first big goanna in the land of giant lizards. The wheels whirred and they rocked over rougher ground until it became apparent they would have to go the rest of the way on foot.

Quinn parked the jeep and Nicole clambered out before he could help her. She was absurdly nervous of him, yet exhilarated as well. It seemed a long way up the hill, but the sun struck the top like an ancient temple.

'All right, little one,' he turned to face her, 'let's see what you're made of.'

'There are footholds, I hope?' she asked breathlessly.

He didn't answer but put out his hand and she took it, a little spellbound. Ten minutes later he made her rest, his jewelled glance a little wry on her lovely flushed face. Then when she nodded to go on he drew her after him, half lifting her, sheltering her body, her face and her hair from whipping branches and lavender-flowering shrubs that prickled. At last, almost at the top, he swung her up before him so she had first sight of the mighty, lonely landscape.

Her heart was pounding and she felt a little like collapsing, but the view was unbelievable and it confronted her on every side. She was so spent but elated she had to shelter in the curve of Quinn's arm, trying to get her breath back and half laughing with the effort.

'It's incredible!' she said, like a peace-offering. 'Surely the Earth Mother was born here?'

'Get your breath back!' he ordered, though she could see she had pleased him.

Nicole half turned her head and drew in her breath. The wild beauty of that vast panorama was breathtaking for so many reasons: the great size and the limitless horizons, the brilliant bizarre natural earth colours, the coal fire red of the ridges and sandhills, the dark red of the soil, the yellow gold of the luxuriant grasses, the dark green of trees and bushes, the silver glitter of the maze of waterways, and the man-made lakes, and threading the giant tapestry with every imaginable colour, the wildflowers, rejoicing in their short, vivid lives. It was the most wonderful vantage point, like a great uplifted stage. They were left alone now in the whole world with nothing but the primeval land and the deep silence. It was enough to fire anyone's blood, yet it was curiously humbling.

Unaware, Nicole was still resting against him, her breath coming rapidly. 'I wouldn't have missed this for the world. The silent kingdom.'

'So you *do* understand a little,' he said abruptly.

'No!' The swift colour ran into her cheeks. 'I understand a lot. You really look to be disappointed in me.'

'Maybe I do!' he agreed briefly. 'When you're rested we'll go down.'

'Surely not for a while. You've brought me all this way.' He had moved away from her and she found herself swaying a little.

'Maybe I want to discuss one or two things.'

'Please, no!' She held out an appealing hand. 'I won't let you spoil this for me. It's been so wonderful.'

'Still anxious to have Wayne paint you?' he persisted, leaning back and lighting a cigarette.

'Why not? Some good might come of it. For Wayne, I hope.'

'That would be a miracle indeed!' His blue eyes slid over her. 'You understand, don't you, that Wayne is talented but not much more?'

Nicole turned away from the awe-inspiring view to face him. 'Why don't you give him a chance?' she said a little recklessly.

'You mean let him come?'

'Why should it disturb you?' she challenged him.

'You think it a good idea to let him get all excited about painting a beautiful woman?' he asked caustically.

'I was only trying to help. He seems to be absorbed in his painting.'

'It would be a vast improvement if he was absorbed in supporting himself. If you think I'm going to let him paint you by day and make love to you in the evening you're very much mistaken.'

By now Nicole had almost forgotten the view. 'You beast!' she exclaimed excitedly.

'Actually I told him *no*!' Quinn broke in, and pitched away his cigarette as though it had suddenly developed a bitter flavour. 'You might find it amusing to make another conquest, but just watching it would make me ill!'

She flushed scarlet. She knew she did. Damn him for everything! To bring her to such a lonely, intoxicating spot, to falsely accuse her. . . . She made a dive past him and though his long arm shot out she precipitated herself upon the steep descent. Tiny turquoise blue wildflowers that grew in their thousands scattered all over her hair and lithe branches thrashed out to enfold her slender, graceful body. She heard him call after her with hard, commanding urgency, but she fought out of her confines, the sunlit world reeling in a red haze of anger. Pebbles were rolling under her feet and her heart leapt with fright as she lost her footing and fell backwards, grabbing at a branch that slid through her fingers and burnt her. She cried out in the urgency of panic, then a hard hold on her flailing hand brought instant pain. Her irresistible momentum was stopped and he pulled her twisting body back, clamping his arms around her, concentrating grimly on keeping them both from falling headlong.

She was scarcely able to breathe, appalled by the realisation that she had brought them both to the brink of danger. Her arm was aching as though he had pulled it from its socket and his hold on her body was brutally strong. Shock took her breath and kept her trembling and useless, but after all he succeeded in keeping them both clamped to the rock face.

It seemed like an eternity, but it was all over in seconds. His face when she dared lift her head was pale beneath its dark tan, his eyes so glittery they might have been inanimate gems. 'Why?' he asked so contemptuously she almost cried.

'I'm sorry!'

He laughed with black humour. 'You could have killed yourself, you little fool!'

'*Both* of us!' She ran out of words and began to shake uncontrollably.

'Next time you mightn't be quite so mindless!' Quinn still held her, but he gestured towards the top of the ancient ironstone formation. 'You couldn't cope with the physical task of descending. You need time to get over your fright.'

'I'm all right!' she gasped, but her body was shaking with reaction.

'Up you go!' He ignored her, keeping a hard hand at her back.

Safely on the summit, she let her weakness take over, falling limply to the ground and closing her eyes. She caught one glimpse of Quinn standing over her, so strong and arrogant he made her feel doubly stupid and frail. The blue-flowered scented bushes protected her face from the sun, but still she put a hand over her eyes as though more than the sun was threatening her. She had never felt so vulnerable in her life.

'Stop that shaking!' he felt impelled to say.

'Damn it, I feel so wretched!'

'I have to take a lot of the blame. I was trying to upset you.'

'You've never wanted me here, have you? Not even now.'

'Especially not now!' He was beside her, gathering her waiting body into his arms. 'You know I want you, don't you?'

'You make it sound as though you hate yourself for it,' she muttered.

'Does it hurt you?' His pale blue eyes were sweeping every inch of her face and body.

'No more than being tortured or buried alive.'

'Little fool!' His caressing hand encircled her throat. 'If you want to find happiness you need to find wisdom. I could only hurt you, turn you into a frightened child. I'm going to drive you back to the city, if I have to. You'll grow there where you could never withstand this savage land.'

His hand when it shaped her breast shocked and aroused her so she cried out to him, half lifting her body towards him, remembering the way it had been the last time he had held her and made love to her without love.

Though it filled her with sorrow she could find no way to resist him, as though he had taught her all she would ever need to know about storm-ridden desire.

The light through the screening shrubs was a golden halo behind his head and she linked her arms behind his head as his mouth found hers like a long-exiled lover. Passion kindled like a torch set to spinifex. She could never outlive the memory of sensation, not even if her life spanned more than a hundred years. They were resting together, Quinn's body half covering her own, his mouth taking hers with an uncontrolled hunger, the touch of his hands on her innocent body so greatly exciting, she lost her will to deny him his ravishing little cruelties. Her heart was unguarded as her body was from invasion. She couldn't fight him because she loved him—a terrible retribution for having led Peter to mortal recklessness.

'You should have been a witch!' he muttered fiercely against her creamy throat. 'An enthralling little witch who could rob a man of his strength and purpose.'

'Just love me!' she whispered without realising the naked longing on her face. Her sensitised breasts were aching, her body intolerant of the least cessation in his lovemaking. She had never in her life imagined she could act with such abandon, but she was thirsting, and hungry for a blazing togetherness she could remember all her life ... longing to be only one of his possessions if he wanted it that way for her senses had left her.

He kissed her then until she was afraid she would faint, so turbulent were the sensations he was releasing in her. She couldn't even feel the warm, hard ground beneath them or the bruises on her own body. Then, like a stunning, bewildering rejection, he released her and sat up abruptly, winning a clear victory over his own desires and her woman's skills at sorcery.

Men were the mighty ones, she thought wildly, though

she couldn't move. Weak, loving women were always left with a storm of crying. Quinn Rossiter was determined on being master of his own destiny and it could never include a woman who only fired his blood until his skin burned with the heat. For the rest, she had to lie there with her dark hair tumbled around her until she felt strong enough to descend to the plain.

CHAPTER EIGHT

WHEN they arrived back at the homestead, Christine's face appeared at an upstairs window, then in the next minute she was hoisting herself out into the sunshine waving her arms excitedly above her head.

'Great news, great news!'

'Suppose you tell us,' Quinn invited calmly.

'Val's had her baby. A son!' Tears sprang into her radiant blue eyes. 'That makes Mamma a grandma, me an aunty and you and Kim uncles for the first time.'

'That's wonderful!' Nicole met her friend's excited eyes. 'And they're both well?'

'According to Mamma's message, yes. I guess the whole Outback will know. It went on the air about twenty minutes ago.'

'I guess they will!' Quinn smiled and ruffled his sister's lemon curls. 'Surely this calls for a celebration?'

'Oh, I'm so *thrilled*!' Christine cried unnecessarily. 'Mamma can relax now, so can Val and Rob. Just fancy, my own little nephew. Mamma will spoil him like mad.'

'Did she say when she was coming home?' Quinn asked.

'As soon as Val's out of hospital. She'll have a job tearing herself away, but Rob has a big family and his mother must be marvellous. She'll keep her eye on Val. When the little man's a bit older Val's promised she'll bring him home so we can all have a look at him.'

'Which means friends and family from thousands of miles around!' Quinn smiled. 'All right, get off a message of our own.'

'I already have,' said Christine with a burst of laughter. 'They'll be beating the drums from here to the Territory. Oh, come inside, both of you,' she threw her arms around both of them with a wonderful happiness in her pretty face, 'we'll have a cup of tea now and tonight we'll break out the champagne!'

The girls were swimming in the homestead pool when Margot arrived. Neither was amazed to see her because Margot used every excuse to fly in to Sapphire. Val's baby offered a perfect opportunity to share in the celebrations and she declared herself as thrilled as anyone.

'Who drove you back to the house?' Christine pulled on her flowered robe.

'Paddy!' Margot turned and frankly inspected Nicole's slender figure. 'Hadn't you better get out of the sun?' she queried, with a supercilious lift of her eyebrows.

'I'll dry off first,' Nicole returned pleasantly, 'in any case, I don't burn.'

'You don't tan either,' Margot glanced down approvingly at her beautifully tanned bare arms. 'Incidentally, don't you think you owe Wayne an explanation?'

'I'm sorry?' Nicole looked up questioningly.

'Well, you did ask him to paint your portrait.'

'Correction!' Christine swung her legs up on to the redwood recliner. 'Wayne asked Nicole if he could paint her portrait. There's quite a difference.'

Margot's handsome face flushed and she gave a curt nod of acknowledgement. 'All the same, I wonder you found it so easy to put him off.'

'Quinn put him off!' Christine said squarely.

'Quinn?' There was shock and challenge in Margot's angry tone.

'You see, it isn't really convenient,' Nicole explained before Christine could throw fuel on the fire. 'What with

Aunt Helen away and Mary confined to her chair.'

'Oh!' From her expression it hadn't even occurred to Margot, but it seemed to offer a more mollifying explanation. 'It's not as though you're going to continue on as a guest indefinitely!'

'For a guest, we're keeping her pretty busy,' Christine said dryly. 'Why don't you get out of your things and come in for a swim?'

Margot stood up, not even hesitating. 'No, thanks, I'll ride down and join Quinn.'

'Whatever you like.' Christine looked at Nicole and very faintly winked.

'It's all right, I suppose, if I stay overnight?' Margot turned back with the afterthought.

'We'd be delighted to have you,' said Christine smoothly, whatever her true feelings.

'See you later, then.' Margot wriggled her fingers and gave her cool, superior smile. 'I've brought a super dress for the celebration.'

'Has she, damn her!' Christine hissed the moment Margot's tall, athletic form disappeared.

'She walks well,' Nicole observed thoughtfully. 'Head high, shoulders back, very economical in her movements. She's really a very good-looking woman.'

'She knows it, of course, but she's much too commanding a female and she can be a real bitch. I'd keep my eye on her if I were you.'

Nicole shrugged her shoulders and tried a smile.

'I mean it.' Christine wasn't smiling. 'You're the only one I could ever think of to turn Quinn's head.'

For an instant Nicole looked aghast. 'Let's get this all together,' she said wryly. 'I thought you were concerned about *Kim's* being too friendly?'

Christine nodded. 'It's too complicated, I'll admit. I guess beautiful women always act as catalysts. *You* would never choose to hurt anyone, but let's face it, men lose their heads over you. Kim will master his current infatuation when he's obviously not getting any encouragement, but Quinn is something else again. I've seen the way he looks at you now and again. You take care of yourself, hear? Margot might even go in for murder if you took Quinn away from her.'

'I'm no competition!' Nicole hid her eyes behind her huge sunglasses.

'Stop underestimating yourself!' Christine warned, and sat up for emphasis. 'I don't want anyone or anything to hurt you any more, not even the brother I adore. If you think you're not able to reach Quinn you're kidding yourself. You're not just lovely to look at, you're much, much, more. Just having you here has been terrific. You've even got Roz to trust you. The way you manoeuvred them both out today left Kim thinking he intended it all along. They'll get together again, don't worry. Kim will realise he was never in the running. In fact, he was selling himself a daydream. It's Quinn you care about, isn't it?'

'Yes.' The word just slipped out, not joyously, but flatly.

'I thought so,' Christine nodded shortly. 'There's nothing I could want more than to have you in the family, but Quinn's so controlled, so disciplined, he could hurt you.'

Nicole shifted her position a little out of the hot sun. 'Sometimes I wonder if I was born to trouble!' she sighed.

'It's part of being a woman!' Christine smiled.

'Aside from that, we both know *my* kind of woman wouldn't fit into any of Quinn's plans.'

'Meaning Margot's more his style.'

'Exactly. She's eminently suitable to play mistress of a great station.'

Christine shook her fair head very gently. 'Not altogether. I think you'd find most of the staff see her as
an arrogant bitch, and I can't really blame them. She
really does bung on the Miss Rossiter bit and she's not in
the least kind or imaginative. You'll find the kids never
wave to her the way they wave to you, and the housegirls
keep right out of her way!'

Nicole thought about it and found she had to agree.
'Yes, she can speak very sharply, but heavens, isn't her
voice honeyed with Quinn?'

'Just keep looking over your shoulder!' Christine
warned, and her voice sounded solemn. 'It isn't hopeless
with you and Quinn. According to all the legends, even
the gods were susceptible to a siren's call.'

'Susceptible, yes, but Quinn's hard enough and smart
enough to know exactly what he wants.'

Christine nodded and reached for her long, frosty
drink. 'It's not easy, I'll admit. There's a rage in him
against a particular kind of woman.' She shook her head
slowly. 'It's sad, sad, sad, and it happened a long time
ago.'

Nicole understood more when late in the afternoon Margot asked her to look around the art collection together.
She seemed in an uncharacteristically friendly mood and
if Nicole was surprised by the invitation and the laughing
explanation that Margot couldn't really see anything in
paintings, she shrank from offending the older girl. They
walked along the gallery with Nicole offering her gentle
but informed opinions, and Margot's long hazel eyes slid
from one painting to the next without really seeing anything. She was really, as she claimed, a Philistine in the
art world, even as she was aware that Quinn had added
considerably to a family collection spanning several
generations.

'You sound just like Wayne!' Margot laughed with no real amusement. 'God knows where he got his arty streak.'

'Surely from the Rossiters?' Nicole indicated the long lined walls of beautiful and valuable paintings. 'They surely were, and are, art connoisseurs.'

'Well, there is money in it!' Margot commented, 'and they've always shown a great deal of interest in that!'

Nicole accepted this silently, then as she went to walk on, Margot suddenly grasped her arm, some kind of curious excitement communicating itself to Nicole. 'I fancy no one's ever shown you the portrait of Marianne?'

'No——' Nicole's voice died away.

'Come along and I'll show you. It's in the attic.'

'I'd rather not.'

'For heaven's sake!' Margot laughed again and it sounded a little wild. 'What are you afraid of, a lurking ghost?'

'To be truthful I'd prefer to be shown it by one of the family,' Nicole told her.

'And I'm *not*?' Margot accused sharply.

'You know what I mean. I feel such a picture might be very personal and private.'

'You bet it is! That's why it's all sealed up in the attic. In the early days poor old Helen needed all the self-confidence she could muster. Not that *she* put it there, Cousin Carl did that, but he couldn't bring himself to slash it—more's the pity! That woman did a lot of damage.'

'She must have had a bad time of it herself,' Nicole offered huskily, always compassionate.

'What rubbish!' Margot drawled, and her voice sounded deadly. 'I know you're interested for all your efforts to hide it. Come on up.' She turned slowly, still keeping her grip on Nicole's arm. She was very strong and cunning, like a cat intent upon a mouse, and she fully intended that Nicole should see the painting of the woman who had so cruelly broken a husband's and a small boy's hearts.

Nicole had no idea where they were going. The house was very big and a lot of the rooms were shut up and un-used except for the odd occasion when the whole clan gathered. 'Poor Nicole!' Margot's hazel eyes flashed strangely. 'You've gone quite pale, did you know?' She pulled Nicole up a short flight of stairs, then slowed and stopped before a door. 'Here we are!'

She went in and Nicole followed, dismayed to feel her heart pounding. Dust lay everywhere like a disease and she noted in the soft burning light and long shadows that there was old furniture pushed against the walls, trunks and tea chests, a great pile of books and more than a dozen paintings in large frames, and occupying an easel covered by a throw-over of violet velvet, what would seem to be a painting of conspicuous size.

Margot shook the velvet free with her surprisingly strong hands and Nicole, looking up, saw a girl in a gold satin dress, a girl beautiful enough to make her gasp, the dark eyes brilliant and steady, white skin glowing like alabaster, the dark hair springing back from a perfect widow's peak. The background was a dark green with just the suggestion of light, and Nicole leaned towards the painting without blinking an eyelash.

'I'm sure I've never seen anyone more beautiful,' she said.

'Yes.' Margot's long fingers on the gilt frame trembled slightly. 'You do see the resemblance, don't you?'

'No.' Nicole continued to look up at the spirited patrician face. The bone structure was perfect, but the look in the girl's eyes made her feel immensely sad. 'Quinn, I think, is the image of his grandfather. Then there's the Rossiter blue eyes. Startling eyes.'

'I'm not talking about Quinn!' Margot said harshly.

'Then who?' Nicole twisted her head to meet Margot's eyes.

'Oddly enough, you!' Margot snapped the word off. 'You must see you're much of a type.'

'We have the same colouring,' Nicole ventured, 'but I feel insipid beside Marianne.'

'Maybe so,' Margot agreed maliciously, 'but still, there's a marked resemblance. Mostly, I think, in the very dark hair and white skin. You completely miss out on Marianne's fatal sex appeal.'

'It didn't do her much good!' Nicole said reflectively. 'I wonder what went wrong?'

'It was the way she was brought up!' Margot stated bluntly. 'To a woman used to parties and people, everlasting admiration, all the entertainments a big city can offer, Outback life must have seemed like a prison. Obviously too she had hot blood in her veins, and with a man busy for so much of the time, the break-up was inevitable.'

'It seems more like a tragedy. I do know Quinn's mother never married again, yet his father found happiness and fulfilment in his second marriage.'

Margot laughed shortly and without pity. 'Believe me, my dear, *that* blow to his pride nearly killed him. You didn't know Quinn's father. He was never a happy man. A strong man, a hard man, a powerful man, but never a happy one. Helen did her best, but it was like mating a wren with an eagle.'

Nicole spoke with difficulty, dismayed by Margot's disloyalty to the woman who had shown her nothing but courtesy and open-handed hospitality. 'I'm sure you're being unfair to her. Helen is a born homemaker and she must have been very pretty and lovable as a girl. Chris and Kim are very cheerful, balanced people. They couldn't have known an unhappy home life, no matter what you say.'

Margot's gold-flecked eyes were hard and glittering. 'You're an absolute fool, aren't you, but then I'm forgetting you know nothing about the family. Tell me, whose idea was it getting dear little Rosalind over?'

Nicole's purely cut features reflected her distaste. 'Why wouldn't I want to meet Kim's close friend? Roz is a nice girl. I like her very much.'

'Yes, a sweet child!' Margot spoke with contemptuous vigour. 'I suppose you really counted on being able to seduce one or other of them, Kim or Quinn.'

Nicole flushed scarlet, sickened by Margot's ugly, harsh manner. 'I know you don't like me,' she said in a low controlled voice, 'you've shown that pretty clearly from the first time we met, but there's no excuse for being so offensive.'

'Yes, how ghastly, how unjust!' Margot mocked her, a strange flame in her eyes. 'By the way, I had a good long talk with a friend of yours, Agnes Vaughn.'

Despite herself, Nicole shuddered uncontrollably. 'How *dare* you!'

'A woman of strong opinions, Mrs Vaughn,' Margot continued mercilessly. 'She's convinced you're a criminal.'

'I shall always blame myself!' Nicole whispered in a pitifully small voice.

'I should think so!' Margot pressed her advantage. 'I heard all about Peter and how much he loved you. The cruel way you threw him over, and how he took his own life.'

'I'm sure he never meant to kill himself,' Nicole cried, though her face was colourless. 'Anyone who knew him always said he drove much too fast.'

'Well, whatever it was,' Margot interrupted dryly, 'his mother blames you and so do a lot of people.'

'No, that's not right!'

Margot came close to her and looked her straight in the eyes. 'It would be an awful thing to have to tell Quinn.'

'Why should you?' Nicole protested, though her heart felt like lead.

'Quinn would never look at a woman who was little more than a murderess. I don't think we ought to tell him, do you? He wouldn't understand.'

'Perhaps not!' Nicole muttered in a same, lifeless tone. 'You're a very ruthless person, aren't you?'

'I haven't got a man's death on my conscience!' Margot exclaimed angrily. 'I've no wish to upset and embarrass you, but I'm telling you plainly to leave Quinn alone.'

'Such a warning isn't necessary!' Nicole burst out, almost desperately.

'Isn't it?' Margot's thin mouth tightened. 'He's adopted a mighty funny attitude about Wayne's painting you.'

'I *told* you, it isn't convenient.'

'He told me, too, but you're forgetting I know Quinn. He flatly refused to discuss the subject further. I've got a few brains, you know, and I'm long used to cutting out the competition. It was a simple matter to track down your background—in fact I put a man on it. It took a few dollars more than I expected really, but in the end I believe it will be well worth it. Mrs Vaughn, when I contacted her, was only too pleased to talk. She's even worked up a real hatred for your father. But his being an important man in the city won't help you out here. Mrs Vaughn gave me the full benefit of her hatred and hysteria. How were you ever dumb enough to get mixed up with such a crowd anyway?'

'And you?' Nicole asked, and lifted her head. 'What would you call yourself?'

Margot cut her short, swinging on her in a fury, grasping her shoulder with hard, hurting fingers. 'I'm a woman, who'll do anything to keep her man.'

'And be justified?'

'Yes!' Margot's breathing was loud and noisy.

'Then control yourself!' Nicole shook herself free of that punishing grip. 'Immediately Mrs Rossiter gets home, I'll leave.'

'I suggest you leave before then!' Margot gritted, and walked with her swift stride to the door. 'You don't want to destroy what little respect the family have for you.'

'The family know,' Nicole whispered desolately, because she could scarcely talk.

'But not Quinn!' Margot's eyes travelled from the beautiful, adored girl in the painting to Nicole's trembling figure. 'White magnolias, both of you, but definitely losers!' She broke into a laugh that was viciously sarcastic. 'Do what I tell you, Miss Lindfield, and your little secret is inviolate. But if for some reason you decide to be reckless, I'll turn over my file to Quinn. He's nothing if not hard on women who use men deliberately!' Margot went out the door and banged it heavily after her.

In the sudden draught, dust rose in flat rings to constrict Nicole's throat. She coughed until she choked and the weak tears of reaction sprang to her eyes. Above her head the beautiful dark eyes of the portrait looked out brilliant and undisturbed. Marianne was free now of all life's problems and heartaches, but Nicole felt she had been returned to her nightmare. For Margot to have gone to such lengths to discredit her! It seemed perfectly dreadful and an example of human vindictiveness. She was too overwrought, too horribly caught up in all her old guilt feelings to think clearly. She only knew she couldn't bear that Quinn should hear the whole tragic story and blame her. Mrs Vaughn's poisoned denunciation would live with her for ever.

Fatalistically, she dragged herself to the door, pulling on the old, heavy knob. It came away in her hands, and she gazed down at it almost in a stupor. Obviously it had been broken for a long time. She felt sick and made an effort to calm herself. If she couldn't open the door from this side, and after a few feverish attempts, she found that she couldn't, she would have to begin pounding in the hope that someone would hear her. It seemed certain now that Margot had pulled the door deliberately, hoping to frighten her or at least put her to the horrible embarrassment of calling. This was a private place, she knew that quite well, and she was not connected with the family—certainly not close enough to be able to unveil Marianne's portrait and stare at it with curiosity. But she had not felt curiosity, had she, but sadness and fascination.

She went to the door and began pounding on it, acutely and horribly aware that her being there alone might convey a vulgar curiosity that had never been intended. Margot was extraordinarily strong and she had as good as pushed her to the attic. With her hands sore and rigid she waited and listened. In another minute or two she would begin again. Margot could not possibly leave her here, and with a celebration dinner to prepare Christine and Rosalind would be looking for her support. Spending much more time in this curiously haunted attic seemed heart-chilling, but as she turned back to look into Marianne's beautiful, melancholy eyes the feeling of near-hysteria passed. Perhaps Marianne was showing her the way? To protect herself from a lifetime of acknowledged heartbreak, she would have to go away. To be at Quinn's mercy when she loved him so much was to invite evocation of all the old disasters.

She subsided on to an old velvet cushion on the ground, leaning her head forward on her knees. Sooner or later they would search the attic.

Nicole was actually shivering all over when they found her, though the air was anything but chilly. Quinn threw open the door, his tall, powerful form silhouetted blackly against the weak glimmer of the lights on the stairway. She didn't know how she looked with tears in her eyes and a streak of dust across one cheek, but he lifted her bodily with brutal strength born out of some fear. Christine and Rosalind were both looking anxious behind him and she held out her hand to them lest she slide into a faint.

'What in God's name are you doing here?' Quinn reacted violently.

Nicole tilted back her head to stare at him, receiving the warmth and power of his body. 'The door shut on me and I couldn't get it open.'

'Nicky dear, we've been so worried!' Christine's eyes dilated over the portrait and back to Nicole's rapt face. 'Come away now!'

'I'm sorry.' She had to rouse herself to give an explanation. 'When it became apparent I couldn't open the door from the inside I pounded and pounded, but none of you heard.'

'We thought you were outside,' Rosalind said nervously. 'Margot thought she saw you slip out into the garden. You seem to like those lilies that grow down near the lake.'

Quinn had his black head flung up, looking at his mother's portrait in an unbreathing stillness, the power of his arms holding Nicole quiet and silent. There was no comfort in his arms but a ruthless possession; no love, but a lifetime of pain. Yet her body yielded, because it was too difficult not to.

'Oh, darling, what did you want up here?' Christine very nearly wailed.

'It's not like that, Chris, please believe me.'

Rosalind's small face looked touchingly concerned. 'Thank heavens you're all right. Listen, I'll go down and tell the others we've found you.'

'Thanks, Roz.' Christine turned to pat her on the shoulder. 'There's so much to do I'd better go too. Don't worry about getting dinner tonight, Nick, Roz and I should be able to manage and Mary wants to help, though she's still a bit stiff and sore.'

Both girls had gone before Quinn spoke to her again. 'Was it worth it?'

She winced and gave a little protesting moan, but still he didn't release her. 'I had no intention of intruding. I didn't even know the portrait was here.'

'But you've seen it now, and you've paid for your curiosity.'

'Is it so dreadful?' Pleadingly she caught at his arm.

'You don't move until you tell me what you were up to.'

She laughed until she couldn't laugh any longer without risking his striking her with cold, clinical resolution. 'Stop that!' he ordered curtly, and jerked her to attention.

If possible the blue blaze of his eyes was making her even more desperate. 'I'm sorry if I've offended you, angered you. I know I have. I wasn't prying, believe me— I simply didn't think. The room was here so unexpectedly at the top of the stairs, I just walked in.'

'And that's the truth?' He put out his hand and she felt his fingers travel with sureness and authority over the bones of her face.

Bewildered, moved, unable to control the desperate passion he aroused in her, she leaned her cheek against his hand with such yearning she couldn't have told him more clearly that she loved him.

'Nicole?' In the urgency of the moment it seemed to both of them he was about to sweep her up into his arms, but Margot's warning made her dark eyes flash and her body go rigid as if he both excited and terrified her.

'Please, Quinn, let me go!'

'Why not?' he said harshly. 'For one thing I'm a fool to be so violent and drastic. Run away, little girl, while you still can.'

He let go of her and she staggered, staring into his eyes. 'With Aunt Helen coming home, there's nothing more to keep me here. I've had a wonderful holiday. I can't thank you enough.'

'Oh, shut up!' he said roughly, lifting his black head with characteristic arrogance. 'When do you want to go? Straightaway, this week? Let's get it fixed now.'

'I hate you!' she wailed so desperately it sounded tragic.

'I know!' Quinn turned about to look down at her. 'You hate me better than anyone in the world.'

She didn't answer, because there was no answer. If he put out his hand he knew she would go to him. She shivered and drew herself taut, defensiveness in every line of her slender body. 'Nobody knows better than I do what I really feel, and I'm still going.'

He moved then in silence, covering the beautiful, romantic portrait, draping the velvet over the elaborately carved gilded frame. When he had done this he turned to her briefly, the barrier between them not only in her imagination but the hard reality of his voice. 'It's better you should,' he said with such finality Nicole regained the use of her trembling limbs. Her deep hurt, her hopelessness, what was left of her pride, gave her feet wings. She streaked down the stairs, finding her way back into the gallery, and from there to her room, not even aware she was crying convulsively. There were no defences she could hide behind now. She had allowed herself the bitter sweet luxury of showing Quinn her love and yearning, yet he couldn't have more effectively shut her out. Let Margot do her worst. She *had* to go away now.

When Christine knocked on the door there was no answer. She opened it and looked in, seeing Nicole huddled on the bed, her face buried in the pillows, to muffle the sound of her weeping.

'Nicky darling, don't cry like that!' Christine flew across the room to put her arm around her friend. 'What on earth's the matter? Please tell me.'

Nicole turned round and sat up trying to cover her hot, distorted face. 'Oh, God, Chris!'

'What *is* it?'

'Aren't you sick of me? I'm such a fool, and I bring trouble not only on myself but on everyone who cares for me.'

Christine sat down on the side of the huge fourposter, pushing her friend's tumbled hair away from her desperate tear-stained face. 'You're too hard on yourself, you always were. It was Margot who took you up to the attic, wasn't it?'

'What's the use of discussing it?' Nicole sighed exhaustedly.

'It was a detestable thing to do!' Christine burst out heatedly. 'She always was a bully and she knew perfectly well the door won't open from the inside.'

'Quinn was very angry.' Nicole had stopped crying and she dashed the last of her tears from her face. 'I've told him I'll be leaving just as soon as I can.'

'I don't see why there's any need for you to do that!' Christine looked back at her with dismay. 'You're only just settling in to the place and I'd miss your company dreadfully. Besides, what will Mother think with your tearing off like that?'

Nicole smiled a little bitterly. 'The party's over, Chris. Margot knows all about me.'

'What the devil is there to know?' Christine asked with bewilderment. 'You're of excellent family and character.'

'I couldn't take it, Chris,' Nicole muttered, not looking at her friend. 'Margot has been checking on me quite a lot. She's really a very unpleasant and destructive woman. She even went to the incredible length of contacting Peter's mother.'

'I don't believe it!' Christine whispered aghast. 'Not even Margot would do that. Why, it's positively vicious —and such colossal cheek? How dare she! What possible business is it of hers?'

'She's threatened to tell Quinn.'

'Oh yes, she'd love that. She'd probably like to tear you to pieces with her sharp claws!' Christine said with sombre bitterness. 'She's frightened of you, that's why. She's greedy and possessive and frightened.'

'Why on earth doesn't Quinn marry her and put her out of her misery?' Nicole asked abruptly. 'He's just leading her on, leading her on. No wonder she's nearly mad!'

Christine sighed violently, then got up and began to pace around the soft opulence of the bedroom. 'Perhaps Quinn's never spoken one encouraging word to her. Who's to know? Some people seem to draw an obsessive passion. You're one, Quinn's another. Perhaps Margot's been desperately foolish and we're all wrong. Even if Quinn were to marry her, it would be a marriage of convenience more than a genuine passion. I mean, he's known her all her life and he's done nothing. I've never even seen them hold hands, not that Quinn's one for wearing his heart on his sleeve.'

'He doesn't want me,' Nicole confessed, though it tore away her breath.

'How do you know?' Christine rounded on her. 'Now and again it's seemed to me it looks remarkably like it.'

'No, dear!' said Nicole in a strange tone. 'He told me it's best if I go.'

Christine collapsed silently into a chair, averting her head. 'Can't men be cruel!' she sighed.

'At this very moment I'm convinced of it.'

'So what are we to do?' Christine asked sadly, and with a touch of perversity hurled a cushion across the room.

'Being here has helped me a lot, Chris.' Nicole's pale face in the soft lighting had a shadowy lustre, her dark eyes huge and intense, her hair streaming away from her brow and temples, clinging to the collar of her shirt. 'That's all that really matters.'

'Well, if it has,' Christine asserted, 'you just get dressed and come down to dinner. After all, why do you have to cringe and hide? You've done nothing you have to be ashamed of.' As she was talking she jumped up swiftly and went to the huge walk-in wardrobe. 'Margot has a super dress, has she? We'll see!' Thoughtfully and slowly she ran down Nicole's array of clothes. 'What about this?' She emerged from the wardrobe with a long, beautiful scarlet silk dress over her arm. 'If you're supposed to be the wicked lady, you might as well have a bit of fun!'

'Better not, Chris,' Nicole said awkwardly, and brushed a drying tear from her cheek. 'I don't want your celebration evening to turn into a nightmare.'

'I don't care,' shrugged Christine. 'Just let her try anything. I'm not as ladylike as you, dear. It might be Margot who'll finish up feeling sorry for herself.'

'I doubt it,' Nicole answered forlornly. 'She hates me and she's determined to humiliate me. In fact she thinks nothing at all about it. She told me quite plainly she'd do anything to keep Quinn.'

'I don't care what she says!' Christine breathed, holding the scarlet silk dress against her. 'Quinn *couldn't* have such atrocious taste. The kind of man Margot really wants is a lapdog to trot around after her. Just whistle and he'll run. She doesn't realise it, of course, she's had her heart and her mind fixed on Quinn for so long.' Turning away from her own reflection, she glanced back at Nicole. 'What about splashing your face with cold water and coming down to help us get dinner? You're a better cook than all of us put together and Mary gave a cry of despair when I said you were lying down with a bad head.'

Hearing this, Nicole dragged herself up from the bed. 'It's a mistake for Mary to try to do too much too soon!'

'That's exactly what I told her.' Reverently Christine draped the beautiful red dress across the end of the bed. 'You're going to look fabulous in that, I know it.'

Nicole's heart was still beating quickly and uncomfortably. 'It's too bare for a family dinner party,' she protested.

'No, it's wonderful. The sort of dress I'd like to wear and I can't. You'll look like some beautiful dark temptress, enticing and enchanting, enslaving at a glance!'

'You're crazy!' Nicole said wryly. 'If you knew how I felt!'

'Anything is possible!' Christine offered with a smile. 'Quinn might sweep you up into his arms and carry you off to some desert hideaway.'

'He might,' Nicole murmured in a soft, husky voice, 'but he doesn't love me. Hunger isn't love, and he could tear the heart from my body. No, Chris,' she said plaintively, and moved off to the adjoining bathroom, 'life's a mess!'

The formal dining room looked dazzling under the light of the magnificent cathedral chandelier, the dark panelled walls hung with paintings, a superb Victorian mirror surmounting the carved fireplace, reflecting the spectacular chandelier, the furniture dark and heavy in the Victorian style but quite in keeping with the scale of the room, the long polished dining table seen at its best when enhanced by fine crystal and bone china and some notable family silver. Georgian silver gleamed too from the massive sideboard, looking extraordinarily rich and decorative against its sombre background, and all four young women who sat around the magnificently polished table were made to look more beautiful and delicate against such a superb background.

'*Squisito!*' Kim pronounced after each course, while Rosalind smiled at him, her eyes shining with love. Christine had lent her a turquoise dress and it did wonders for her expressive eyes, tingeing the grey with blue and lifting her hair and her skin.

'A combined effort!' Nicole smiled, and Rosalind gave her a grateful look that held more than a glint of admiration. In what time they had, Nicole had decided on asparagus milanese, tournedos cut from prime beef fillet and served with a delicious mushroom sauce, a combination side salad tossed with vinaigrette until every crisp green leaf was glistening and because Kim always insisted on his favourite vegetable, tiny new potatoes tossed in butter with fresh herbs. As a dessert, Nicole had made use of Mary's beautiful, light chocolate sponge, transforming it into a rich, luscious gateau by layering and filling and decorating. Rosalind had watched avidly, because once she saw how, she was determined to try the same thing herself. She couldn't remember when she had enjoyed a dinner more in her life, washed down by excellent wine, in Sapphire's splendid dining room with Kim's chair opposite her own. It was wonderful, so naturally Rosalind shone.

Margot, in a very plain but sensationally printed sheath, had taken the seat of honour beside Quinn as divine right, every so often sending piercing looks down the table to where Nicole sat to Christine's left and closest to the side door that led back through the house to the kitchen. Margot had not helped with the preparation or serving of the meal, but she had done the flowers exactly as she had been once taught. As each course appeared, she had frowned at it slightly as though she was not altogether sure she could eat it, but in the end, everything disappeared, including a lavish helping of chocolate rum gateau.

Nicole was in the kitchen for a moment when Quinn came through to get the champagne for the toasts. He had scarcely addressed her directly all evening and though her senses rejoiced in the sight of him, so splendidly, infernally elegant, she was determined not to betray the slightest response.

'Leave that!' he ordered, when he saw her briskly stacking some dishes.

'I'm going to, except I dislike too much clutter. The champagne's in the ice bucket.'

'You look very beautiful,' he said in a dry voice.

'Thank you.'

'But don't you want that apron off?'

She was standing away from the central table, obviously poised for flight, and he reached behind her narrow waist to flick away the ruffled apron. 'That's better.' His blue eyes were eloquent over her beautiful feminine body so alluringly revealed by the cling and sweep of the thin, bare dress. 'Oh, how you've changed, Nicole! You look more like I think of you.'

'Does a woman's body horrify you?' she asked with soft sarcasm.

'I don't know if that's exactly how I feel!' he countered sardonically. 'I mean, we knew you had beautiful skin and beautiful hair, but you've always covered up more. Until now!'

'Then don't think you can take advantage of it,' she said sharply, and turned to go.

'You're damned right! There might be hell to pay if I do.'

Back in the dining room, they drank toasts to Valerie and the new baby, then Kim began to make a few amusing toasts of his own. Opposite him, Rosalind bloomed like an iris, her small face alive with reflections of his own uncomplicated enjoyment of the evening. When eventually he lifted his glass to Rosalind she blushed so gloriously it was like an illumination of love.

But not for me, Nicole thought. Never again for me. I must go home. Quinn was looking towards Margot, speaking to her, and she studied his dark profile with something like pain. With his head turned like that, black hair and bronze skin, no one would guess he had brilliant blue eyes. If I give myself enough time, she thought, I can forget him.

When Quinn turned his head back suddenly and flickered a glance at her she couldn't tear her eyes away, not knowing how huge they had gone, how soft and intense. 'I believe they'll be waiting for us to start the corroboree, a thanksgiving ceremony and an entertainment,' he told them. 'Paddy, among others, has spent all afternoon working out the performance and they've invited the women and the young lubras to join them. Mostly in the background, of course, or to one side, but I find their dancing very graceful, especially the hand movements. If you're all ready, we'll go.'

'Where is it to be held this time?' Margot asked languidly.

'Camp one.' Kim held Rosalind's chair. 'It's not going to be a sacred or secret ceremony. The aim is to entertain us and enjoy themselves with no excessive excitement. I heard Quinn extracting that promise. Some of the ceremonies have turned into near-riots.'

'There'll be no riot tonight,' Quinn confirmed crisply. 'Further, they wish to honour the family, Valerie and her new baby. We don't necessarily have to stay for the finish, it could go on for ever, but I suggest we leave now. We'll all fit into the station wagon.'

Margot passed her golden arm around Quinn's sleeve. 'May I sit beside you?'

Her voice was so soft and tender, addressed so tremulously to Quinn's handsome profile, Christine raised her eyebrows derisively and smiled faintly at Nicole. 'Better grab some rugs and cushions,' she said.

'They're already in.' Kim gave his easy, relaxed smile, and caught Rosalind around the waist. 'Let's go!'

The night was brilliantly clear and still and the bush raced darkly by as they made their way to the appointed corroboree ground. Quinn drove with Margot and Christine beside him in the front seat, leaving Kim to sit between the two girls in the back. Although Kim was still as gay and friendly as ever, Nicole had marked a change in his attitude towards her. It was far less personal and more 'family' as though he had discovered anything else would be dangerous. Even now, he still had his arm around Rosalind, but he made no attempt to touch Nicole, not even a brief pressure on her arm as she climbed into the car. She had to admit to a sense of relief even as she lamented that Kim was no longer completely at ease with her. But at least Rosalind was radiant, responding like a wildflower to the rain and the sunlight. It was certainly true that she loved Kim deeply, and it seemed to Nicole, as it did to everyone else, she would make him an excellent wife.

They were beside the Four Mile Lagoon now, and Nicole could see the rings of fire through the trees, sharply orange in the towering darkness and the pillars of trees. She was surprised to find she was trembling with excitement.

'Hey, what's wrong with you?' For the first time Kim touched her bare arm.

Her voice was soft and a little shaky, half way between fervour and laughter. 'I've never seen a corroboree before. It's exciting!'

'You funny little thing, you're trembling!' Whatever his self-imposed restrictions, Kim ran a gentle hand over her hair.

'Let's hope you're not disappointed,' Margot offered in a flat drawl. 'Personally I find a lot of these gatherings a dead bore.'

'Come on, Margot,' Quinn half turned his head, 'you're not committed to go. Would you like me to run you back?'

'Oh, goodness me, no!' Margot said resolutely. 'The dances on Sapphire, especially, are in a very different style from others I've seen, more vigorous and exciting!'

'So you see, Nicky, we don't average out too badly!' Christine said contentedly. 'It's nice that you're excited. We want you to enjoy yourself, and our aboriginal people are among the finest natural dancers in the world. As well as that, their singing and the simple instrument accompaniment can be extraordinarily pleasing.'

As they came down on the camp, cries of excitement and welcome rang out on the bewitching, starlit night.

A group of dancers, their bodies brightly painted in
ochres, brilliantly coloured parrots' feathers round their
heads and bunches of leaves tied to their wrists and their
ankles, moved away from the glowing orange radiance of
the fires to come forward to greet them. They were almost completely naked except for their loincloths and
their dusky or darkly chocolate bodies glistened with a
burnishing oil.

The leader bowed solemnly to Quinn, who held up his
hand and spoke to them in their own dialect, his resonant
voice vibrating with a special melodiousness. Now the
group retired and in the next few minutes Kim spread the
rugs and cushions so they could take up their positions
opposite the circles of dancers and singers and the
women's group of instrumentalists.

Nicole found herself still standing as though she was
about to join the group of dancers. The blue-scarlet-
orange blaze of the fires was almost hypnotic and she
could see a group of children sitting a little apart, their
great black eyes glistening with pleasure, ready to join
in the clapping and singing though they knew they were
not allowed to jump up and dance. Some of the little
faces she recognised and one child even called to her
until pulled back to attention by a very ancient gin, who
nevertheless was a very important person. The young
lubras had tap sticks and sand drums while the older
women had decorated boomerangs made from a particularly resonant wood. All were arranged in perfect semi-
circles behind the performing males with a tribal elder,
the didgeridoo player, sitting alone as befitting a per-
former of his distinction.

Nicole stood absorbed, her own dress adding exquisite
colour, her white skin glowing against the dark of her hair
and her eyes. The whole scene was infinitely primitive
yet right, the trees curving upwards losing their tops in

the darkness, the blossoming stars glittering in patches. As she turned to find her place a lizard scampered over her sandalled foot and she gave a little distracted cry:

'Oh!'

Quinn half swung around and made a grab for her arm. 'What's the matter?'

She skittered back a little looking down at the ground. 'Something ran over my foot. A lizard, I think.'

'Oh, really!' Margot sighed wearily, 'is that all?'

'It's no laughing matter. I just hope it got away.'

'Yes, ma'am, it has.' Quinn's hand rested lightly at her waist, yet it so disturbed her that her heartbeats quickened and she had to avert her head. 'What little I can do to protect you I shall.' His arm tightened around her and he drew her backwards until they were both seated on the rug and Margot was writhing with resentment. Although Nicole had little to do with this arrangement, for Quinn was at her back so she could almost rest against him, Margot sat as stiff and still as if she had just been stabbed.

A dancer came running into the centre of the clearing and the ceremony began. No longer was the bush silent, for now the didgeridoo throbbed out its strangely compelling message and the rhythm of the tap sticks echoed far around the starlit plains. The slender lead dancer had perfect control, his body slightly bent, his arms and legs moving to the same strong rhythmic beat his ancestors had known. Other dancers joined him, ringing him round, and soon the ballet began to take shape. Quinn had passed on to them that this was to be one of the Dreamtime ballets, enacted in song and dance, with chanting and gestures and, as Nicole saw, considerable interpretative ability. Mother Earth was worshipped by all aborigines, but the stars held them spellbound, inviting a greater reverence. Venus, or Bringah as they called her, was the brightest of all the stars, a great goddess, who appeared in the eastern sky in the morning and the western sky at dusk. Up and up, soaring, hanging in the sky, the Place of Mists, of Lilies, the Blue Lotus, beautiful lotus flower on a stalk, sinking into the ghost gums, brushing the lagoon, going down, down into the Place of Shining Water on Sapphire.

The soft pounding of the sand dunes was hypnotic. The time slipped by in spirit song. An hour ... two ... still the children's hands fluttered like flowers, then came together with perfect precision to match the beat of the women's tap sticks. The beat was so insistent, it seemed to be drumming inside Nicole's quivering body. The whole scene was so vivid, so beautifully barbaric, her everyday inhibitions were banished so that without deliberation, but exhilaration, she rested lightly within the hard curve of Quinn's shoulder as though it would be unthinkable to be anywhere else. Here in the leaping firelight with the air filled with ceremony and chant it was difficult for her to remember to be wise. Her body had no armour, it just fitted Quinn's as smoothly as silk, and as a courtesy he didn't draw away but let her rest and shelter against his hard strength.

One by one the dancers stole away until there were only the lead singer and the musicians left. With a sense of astonishment and returning reality Nicole saw now that under the wondrous headdress of feathers it was Paddy, but a Paddy as she had never seen him: a young man of his tribe, a prince of the Eagle totem. He looked at Quinn, who stood up, drawing Nicole with him. Words came out of Quinn's mouth, but Nicole didn't understand a word of them. Later she was to find out that Quinn had told the boy he was greatly pleased and the re-enactment of the legend was what the spirit of his people needed.

Paddy didn't smile. Nobody applauded as they would

have a white man's performance, but it was apparent to everyone that the ceremony had been a great success, giving honour to the family and strength to the tribes. Paddy turned quietly, lifted his hands to the women and children and immediately they got to their feet, moving like shadows backwards in the direction of the lagoon.

Only then did Nicole find her brain clearing. The ballet had moved her so much she had forgotten to take care. She stood away from Quinn, turning her head with the full realisation that she was being stared at, meeting the yellow glare in Margot's eyes, like a tigress's with a primitive need for revenge. Still Margot spoke to her with an odd calm.

'Did you enjoy that?'

'Very much. It was wonderful!' Nicole's dark head drooped and she touched her temple as though suddenly discovering a pain there.

Christine almost surged up to her, seeing the naked emnity in Margot's eyes. 'I expect you're tired now. Let's go back to the car.'

'Have you a headache, Nicole?' Rosalind asked kindly.

'No.' She tried a smile, but the wave of cold hatred that emanated from Margot's taut body was quickly bringing one on.

None of them spoke much on the way back to the house, and Rosalind's chestnut head pressed happily into Kim's shoulder. From the rigid set of Margot's head Nicole knew full well Margot wouldn't rest until Quinn had been told all about her ignominious past. How foolish she had been to betray herself! Now Margot would never spare her.

They were scarcely inside the house before Margot burst out petulantly, 'I'd like coffee.'

'Does that mean you're getting it?' Christine challenged, and exchanged a look with Nicole.

Margot shrugged her straight shoulders. 'I mean nothing of the sort. Nicole can get it.'

'All right.' Nicole's soft voice was expressionless. She put her hand to her hair again, then murmured in a distressed undertone, 'Oh dear!'

Quinn looked at her and asked dryly, 'What is it now?'

'My earring.'

'And that's a disaster?'

'Yes,' she said huskily. 'My father gave them to me when I got my degree.'

'Yes, I know, sweetie.' Christine frowned, now equally concerned. 'They're quite valuable, aren't they?'

Nicole pulled the other earring off and held it in her hand; a beautiful pearl set in textured gold.

'How foolish you were to wear them!' Margot said sharply like a schoolmistress to a stupid schoolgirl.

'I just forgot. I should have taken them off before we left the house.'

'You had them both on at the end of the performance,' Quinn said with certainty.

Nicole was still standing looking down sadly at the remaining earring. 'Come on,' he said purposefully, 'we'll go back to where we came from.'

'They might be in the car, or in the rugs,' Kim suggested. 'Come and help me look, Roz.'

'Please be careful!' Christine called after them.

Several minutes later after a thorough search Kim and Roz made their way back up on to the veranda where the others were waiting. 'No luck!'

'Have we really got to go searching?' Margot complained.

'Not at all!' Quinn held out his hand to Nicole. 'I've got a good flashlight and we know exactly where to look. Have the coffee waiting for us when we get back.'

'Right!' Christine inclined her head more happily.

'You probably lost it, Nicky, when you went to stand up. I noticed you were rubbing your head.'

'Yes, as if you had a headache,' Rosalind reminded her gently.

They walked over to where the station wagon was parked and Quinn held open the door for her. Nicole huddled into the seat, overcome by a sense of foreboding. Margot's outraged, scowling face had done nothing to comfort her and she felt thoroughly dispirited and unhappy at the loss. She turned her face away as Quinn got in behind the wheel, lifting her hand to the small group on the veranda.

'Don't break down, we'll find it,' Quinn said quietly.

'I hope so,' she sighed.

'If we don't, I'll have another one made for you—an identical match.'

'Please, I wouldn't want you to do that.'

'I'll do it all the same,' he said dryly. 'Give me the other one.'

Her hand touched his own and she shivered. 'Perhaps we'll find it after all.'

From the illuminated dashboard, she saw that it was close upon midnight. When they came to the camp Quinn parked a little distance off from before, coming round to Nicole and holding out an imperative hand. 'Just be careful where you're walking. Keep a little behind me and we'll examine the ground around where we were parked before.'

The light from the torch cut through the darkness flashing here, flashing there, but to no avail. The grass, embroidered with paper daisies, had been flattened by the heavy tyres exactly marking their first parking spot, but no gleaming pearl was picked up by the powerful flashlight.

'I've lost it, I just know I have,' Nicole sighed.

'Get up!' He flashed the light over her kneeling figure. Her skin was dazzling in the light and her hair was tumbled across one check. 'I told you it isn't a disaster. I'll get you another.'

She took his hand and he pulled her to her feet. 'You're a fool, Nicole, you're trembling.'

'Well, what if I am?' She whirled away from him, always vulnerable, her heart beating fast and her blood hot in her veins. 'We haven't looked down in the clearing.'

'Did you think I didn't mean to, or was coming back here just an excuse to get you to myself?'

'I don't believe that's what you wanted.'

'Even when you look like a tongue of flame?'

'Please, Quinn, I can't see without the light.' Her silk dress was rustling softly and as he came nearer he could see the pulse in her white throat.

'All right,' he said vibrantly, 'though I expect you to say thank you if I find it.'

The fruit of the emu apple looked startlingly bright in the torchlight, small and round and hung in feathery branches. Tap sticks and the muffled thud of the sand drum still carried on the night air and the heavy sweetness of boronia was cushioned by honey scent and the fragrance of the little scented lilies that grew in their thousands across the marshes.

Quinn walked ahead of her splashing the light all over the subtly scented earth. Once she skidded on a stone and gave a little mournful cry and he turned back to her half impatient, half amused. 'Don't tell me it's Benny the wonder lizard again?'

Nicole's little alarm had subsided and she stood quite still. 'I wish you'd remember *I'm* wearing high-heeled sandals. It makes walking down grassy slopes a little difficult.'

'Then stay there!' Briefly he spread the bright light over her, then walked on alone, a tall shadowy figure that blended almost immediately with the night.

It was impossible to feel uneasy, for Nicole could still see the flashlight. The night was achingly beautiful and she lifted her head to study the stars in all their glittering splendour. They were extraordinarily brilliant and she didn't wonder that they figured so prominently in all the ancient legends. The uniquely clean sky over Sapphire had great magic and there were all the mighty hunting gods pulsing and glowing to the beat of a celestial drum.

'Quinn?' she called, and it sounded like a happy murmur.

'Sorry, nothing so far!' His voice came back to her.

'This place is bewitching!'

'So you've noticed.'

She moved carefully down the slope, disturbing a few little stones that rattled down into the clearing. 'They're still chanting, aren't they?'

'It will probably go on until dawn.'

She reached him, but his back was towards her while he stared intently at the illuminated ground, making sweeps of the area. 'Didn't I tell you to stay put?'

'It's supposed to be *my* earring!' she retorted.

'And here it is!' he suddenly announced with intense satisfaction. 'No doubt about it. A pearl to match the other!'

She was at the back of him, but he pulled her gently around, holding the circle of light on a flowery carpet of cane grass. The gold glinted in the emerald green, the pearl seemed to blaze. 'Thank goodness we found it!' She went to scoop it up.

'*I* found it!' he corrected firmly. He held her wrist while he retrieved the earring, slipping it into his breast pocket, to join the other one. 'For that matter, how do you know I didn't plant it out here?'

'That's not your style!' she said, smiling faintly.

'We can all be driven to shameful little acts, Nicole. Under the iron I'm as weak as the next man. Maybe I wanted you all alone.'

'You villain!' There was a little ripple of laughter in her voice.

'Don't denounce me. I didn't plan it at all. That would have been too careless!'

Urgency was running between them and she started back from him lest he shine the torch and see the naked yearning on her face. 'Well, thank you, anyway,' she said.

His voice was wry, wary and mocking all at the same time. 'Why the hell did you have to wear that dress? It's pretty fan-damn-tastic for a simple family dinner!'

'Chris picked it out,' she said apologetically.

'I see. Maybe she wanted something to happen—I don't know.'

'The easy answer is to take it off as soon as I get back to the house.'

'In exchange for what? The flimsy, erotic gear I first saw you in?'

'Surely you're familiar with nightgowns and peignoirs and so forth?' she asked sweetly. 'As for this, I find red cheering myself.'

'It's just the colour to play hell in. How innocent are you, Nicole?'

For answer she walked on, speaking rather angrily. 'Surely *you* don't need to know?'

'I beg your pardon!' There was a smooth, taunting apology in his dark velvet voice. 'I don't like the thought of your ex-fiancé.'

She stood at the top of the rise, her long skirt floating about her feet, the brilliant night sky a backdrop behind her. 'Why not?' she asked faintly. Her blood was racing; she could feel it rushing to her head. Quinn was moving the few paces towards her and the torchlight glanced off his dark, proud face.

'You won't tell me anything about him. What man could trust herself with a woman like you?' He was beside her, looking down at her from his much superior height, and she could sense the hostility in him come burningly alive.

'Haven't you answered that yourself?' she asked crisply. 'Whatever your temptations, the iron nerve remains.'

A night bird suddenly trilled in the trees, startling her so that she turned and ran back to the car, her thick, silky mane swirling about her flushed face, little shooting sparks of anger and excitement in her veins. Quinn was as proud and unyielding as Lucifer, and he would never understand about Peter. She would always be to blame, an inveterate seductress who could only bring a man woe.

She was trying to open the car door when he reached her, his height exaggerated in the glare of the flashlight he set down on the hood. 'Are these some of the games you started practising in the nursery?' he asked crisply.

Nicole only closed her eyes and turned her face away. His hand was over hers on the door handle, and though he wasn't hurting her she couldn't push the button to open the door. 'I want to go back to the house!' she said, with a certain imperiousness of her own.

'Why, Nicole,' he drawled insolently, 'we're both quite aware of what you want.'

'I think not!' She spun around to face him, though in doing so she had placed herself in a position of danger. 'You don't know the first thing about me!'

'Hell!' he laughed beneath his breath. 'All right, go ahead—tell me.'

'It's impossible to talk to you,' she sighed, and tears filled her eyes.

'Pardon me, lady, it's easy. Nothing easier if you'd just tell me the truth.'

'About what?'

'About *you!*' he said with contempt. 'Who the hell else am I interested in? I wanted you from the first moment I saw you.'

'*No!*' her murmured breath denied it.

'My dear,' he caught her against him, threading his hand through her hair, twisting her head back so she couldn't escape him, 'don't pretend. You know full well what you do to me and the best way to do it!'

'And you're not glad at all. You *hate* it!'

'It happens!' he gritted unpleasantly. 'It doesn't seem possible, but I want to keep you and send you away at the same time.'

'Why don't you ask me?' she gasped. 'You seem to think all the situation requires is a decision from you.'

'And why not?' he asked, arrogance written all over him.

'Because *I* mightn't want *you!*' she claimed desperately. 'You're hard and you're ruthless and you shun deep involvement. In a way you're afraid of it, and I'm certainly afraid of you. I knew from the beginning you weren't a man to tangle with, and you're the one who changed that, not me. You never had to kiss me as if I was waiting for it. You never had to try to smash my life. I don't want to be an object of desire, some idiot possession to put up and take down from the shelf. I'm a person with needs and wants of my own.'

'None of which have anything to do with me?' he countered angrily. 'Go on, put me straight.'

The terrible part was she couldn't. She was hopelessly in love with him when he wanted no part of her love. 'Please, you're hurting me!' she whimpered evasively.

'I guess I am!' He relaxed his hold on her only

slightly. 'Which just goes to show I'm not half so controlled as you think!'

'You're conceited!' she gasped painfully. 'Unbearably conceited. A cruel, arrogant male!'

'All three!'

Quinn was angry too, but he wanted her. He bent his head and a soft moan escaped her, a sound that was cut off as his mouth covered hers with an intensity that made her heart give a devastated leap in her breast.

'*No!*' She made one absolute effort to turn her mouth away, but he wasn't going to allow it. His arms were locked around her so tightly she could never hope to escape, the touch of his beautiful, vanquishing mouth so narcotic she was driven to reach up and wind her arms around his neck, spearing her fingers into his crisp vital hair, feeling it spring across her hand.

Craving was cancelling out thought, the desperate need to guard herself against this ruthless invader. No experience in her life had prepared her for Quinn. She should have realised from the beginning he would be able to dominate her completely. Hadn't he tried, instead of making her take all the blame. . . .

Somehow they had moved to the shelter of the car and she was half lying across him, lost in sensation, the dark splendour of being with him, her blood liquid fire in her veins. The touch of his hands on her responsive body was triggering wave upon wave of tumultuous, terrifying yearnings, driving her mad. When he pushed the tiny bodice of her dress away she tried to still the dizzy spinning of her world, but he went on and it seemed so exquisitely right, she lay utterly still accepting his hands as if she was forced to admit now that she was truly made for him.

Her whole body seemed alight and waiting, alluringly yielding, tormenting. . . .

'Did *he* hold you like this?'

The voice was so harsh it couldn't belong to her dream. She opened her eyes and Quinn's head loomed over her. 'Tell me!'

She had to fight to control her reeling mind. 'Who?' she asked weakly.

'This man you fully intended to marry. I don't even know his name. You're determined to keep it from me, and I don't think I could bear to find out.'

It was the moment to speak, to tell him *her* story, but she knew she would live to regret it. It would be a pleasure for Quinn to make her life hell. Yet she loved him, and she was lying in his arms as she never would with another man. Always before she had found it easy to hold part of herself aloof, a goddess dispensing favours, now at least she knew true passion in all its dimensions. There was never a man before Quinn.

As she was thinking it, she was saying it, whispering it over and over, pulling his head down to her, sighing and begging him not to be angry. How beautiful it was to be a woman. She would never regret it.

'Stop me!' he muttered, almost bitterly, against her throat.

'Do you want to?'

'In a moment neither of us will have much choice!' Slowly he drew his hand down the pearly smoothness of her skin. 'Tell me you love me.'

'So you can tell me my love is unreturned?'

'It would be easier to send you away than have you try to escape me. Possibly I might even kill you.' Gently he drew her dark hair across her white throat. 'No, little one, I don't intend anything terrible to happen to you, but if we stay here something surely will. It's always the same, the minute I touch you. Surely that's good enough reason to flee from me?'

Nicole sat up gracefully and kissed the corner of his mouth, that very definite mouth that could so easily melt all her strongest resolutions. 'It's just a dream, isn't it? You only want to caress me. You only want this excitement.'

'Not having known it before I should say that's understandable. You're not most women, Nicole. You're only yourself and damn near irresistible. Let's go back to the house before someone organises a search party.'

Though she smoothed her hair and her dress she knew the natural colour of her mouth and the radiant flame that was in her would betray her. As they walked into the entrance hall Margot almost ran down the stairway, speaking in a hard, demented voice.

'Didn't I tell you you'd regret it?' Her eyes lashed Nicole's beautiful face, instinctively recognising the significance of the subtle change in her appearance; the heavy silken hair that was just faintly tousled, the deepening, darkening eyes, the tender curve of a moulded mouth that was quite without lipstick.

Margot came on down the stairs and as she drew just level with Nicole she threw out her hand with swift strength and caught the side of Nicole's cheek, the fingernail just scoring her temple. 'You bitch!'

Quinn just barely controlled himself, the naked expression on his face frightening to anyone less far gone than Margot. 'Don't indulge your vicious temper here. Do you imagine you can act like that to a guest in my house?'

'A guest only because she hasn't explained herself!' Margot raised terrible eyes to Quinn's face. 'Who would have ever thought *you'd* lose your head over such a heartless and shallow little fraud? Has she told you about Peter? The fiancé she turned out to die when she no longer wanted him? No, Quinn, she has not!'

Curtly Quinn cut her off, putting his outstretched hand on Nicole's shoulder and turning her towards him. 'Do we need all these melodramatics? Who's she talking about?'

'Read it in the file!' Margot cried wildly. 'Women like her are no good. You, more than anyone should realise that!'

'Peter? Peter who?' Quinn asked in a voice that was quite robbed of all expression.

'It doesn't matter.' Nicole turned away from him, hopelessness replacing the soft blaze of her eyes. 'Forget it. It's all over.'

'You're damned right!' Margot moved unsteadily to grasp Quinn's arm, but he thrust her away, staring after Nicole's slender, drooping figure. She seemed to be half dragging herself up the stairs.

'Don't you think I wanted to save you this?' Margot was crying almost wildly.

'*Shut up!*'

Though she heard the rough command, Margot was pitiably unable to stop. 'Haven't you suffered enough through the heartless conduct of your mother? This Nicole is just such a woman, born to bring a man to breaking point. It's crazy, Quinn, to want her.'

'I expect you to clear out in the morning!' he said ruthlessly, swinging on her now in cold anger.

'I just want you to read about her. I left the file in your study!'

'Take it with you and burn it!' he said contemptuously. 'You've never understood me, Margot!'

'Oh, darling!'

Above them in the gallery, Nicole heard the raw anguish in Margot's voice and, strange as it was, she felt a quivering of sympathy. But whatever Quinn's desire for her she knew beyond doubt that he was ready to let her go. Probably when he knew the truth he would come to loathe her. She couldn't find it in her heart to feel hatred or bitterness towards Margot and her vindictive schemes. Though she hadn't meant to, Margot had earned her own separation from Quinn. All the shame and despair had been there in her uttered cry.

The portraits in the long gallery mocked her so that she couldn't control her chattering nerves. She pressed her hand to her smarting check and it felt like hot satin. She was so disorientated the blow hadn't bothered her, nor the murderous rage that had prompted Margot's savage swing. She didn't in the least feel sorry for herself but she was incapable of facing the icy accusation in Quinn's brilliant blue eyes.

Christine would understand why she was leaving, and as she whispered her name desolately, Christine flew up the stairs after her, calling along the gallery, until finally she wrapped her arm around her friend's trembling figure and led her to her room.

CHAPTER NINE

WHEN Wayne rang the house, barely a month after Nicole had returned home, he was the unwitting cause of the greatest surge of hope Nicole had ever known in her life. There was a dinner party in progress, for which she was playing hostess for her father, and Mrs West, her helper behind the scenes, took the call. Of course Wayne had stressed his Christian name, but Nell had whispered smilingly that a Mr Rossiter was on the phone. With her heart pounding violently and her hand shaking so much she was scarcely able to hold the receiver, Nicole first heard Wayne's smooth telephone manner. That was months ago, but the shock remained. However had she been fool enough to imagine it might have been Quinn? Quinn was the sort of man who could ruthlessly cut turbulent emotion out of his life. Quinn, the clear-headed, the iron-willed. But at least he had spared her the terrible compunctions she had known with Peter. Quinn was as steady and hard as granite and no romantic passion for a woman could drive him to despair, let alone tragedy.

Letters from Christine brought news of the family and as she read them a little warmth came into Nicole's eyes, but so far as Quinn was concerned, her sudden departure had brought no great change in his life. Margot had not even been punished, for in her last letter Christine mentioned that the house was full of people, including Margot, Valerie had arrived home with her husband and new baby, and what a great pity it was Nicole couldn't have been there to meet them.

The first time Wayne had come out to the house

172

looking very cool and sophisticated, he had fallen into raptures over her father's collection of modern art, and a few visits later, when he had shown his feelings more, Richard Lindfield had suggested seriously that Wayne could do no better than buy a suitable property and turn it into an art gallery showing the very best of the young moderns, the sort of people who needed genuine help and promotion. As a matter of fact, Nicole's father had pronounced slowly, he knew of just the place, Cornelia Wiseman's old home, rather dilapidated at the moment, but the scene of past grandeurs and present outer-city trendiness.

After that, a lot of things seemed to happen fast. Because Wayne didn't have the kind of money to buy the old Wiseman estate and restore it as well, after a series of discussions with Richard Lindfield, he found an unexpected partner. In a way, art was Richard Lindfield's world as well and he had the shrewd belief that Wayne Rossiter would prove perfect in his new role and capable of building up a successful business. All he needed, Richard Lindfield had assured his daughter thoughtfully, was a firm, guiding hand, and introductions to his new world.

Inevitably her father was proved right, and Nicole was able to observe at close hand the transformation in Wayne. Even his mirror image had changed, for now he was being driven hard by his experienced partner, all his former lethargy had been stripped away. The answer was simple. Wayne loved his work and with hope and purpose he was a different man.

Autumn turned into winter and to keep herself busy Nicole often drove over to Merton Hall to see if she could give Wayne a hand. There was always a small army of workmen surrounding the house, but Wayne had taken it upon himself to restore the interior—a job of work anyone would be bound to admit he was handling extremely well.

Merton Hall wasn't large, but it was an architectural gem and with the amount of money and care that was being lavished upon it, it was simply blooming. Nicole parked her car in the new driveway and stood for a moment admiring the pleasing proportions of the house and the green sweep of lawn. The golden stone walls were offset by all the timber work and the shutters on the upper windows and the lower French doors painted a gleaming white. It all looked very charming and welcoming, and they had decided to call the gallery by its original name, Merton Hall.

Without haste, Nicole walked up the short flight of steps and entered the house. She was going to call Wayne's name, but obviously he had heard her arrive, for he came out into the hallway, struggling to pull protective gloves off his hands. Fine grains of plaster sprayed his hair and his skin and his trendy working gear, but his hazel eyes were shining with health and enthusiasm.

'I thought I'd see you today,' he said smilingly. 'Come and see what I've done.'

'I've just been admiring the place from outside. It won't be so long before you're having your first showing.'

'Marvellous!' Wayne agreed. 'Sometimes I think I'm dreaming, then I see all the nicks out of my hands and I know I'm not. By the way, your father rang earlier on. He's arranged for me to meet Mike Polder.'

'Fascinating!' Nicole smiled. 'You'll get a lot of satisfaction out of showing his work.'

'That's if I can nab him!' Wayne shrugged, and dusted off a chair for her. 'I admire his work tremendously, but he's notoriously difficult to handle.'

'You'll manage!' Nicole let her eyes slip admiringly

around the room, marking all that Wayne had done to restore the lovely moulded and coloured ceiling. He had also lavished a lot of work on the fireplace and the walls had been repapered in a very elegant but unobtrusive design. 'There must be great joy for you in all this,' she said quietly.

'Believe me, there is. I don't think I could ever thank you and your father enough.'

'We believe in you, Wayne,' she said sincerely. 'When you've got the gallery working smoothly you might find time to exhibit some of your own work.'

'Oh no!' Wayne sat down hard in his chair. 'It's better for me to concentrate on discovering and showing real talent. I mean talent like Polder's and that boy Quinn promoted, Jem Roland. I believe his showing went very well. Have you heard from the family?' he asked cautiously.

'I had a letter from Chris the other day.' Nicole watched him thoughtfully.

'Some day she'll see what I can do!' Wayne threw his head back and began massaging the back of his neck.

'Maybe she'd be glad,' said Nicole. 'Have you ever thought of that?'

'No,' Wayne replied at last. 'Chris has never had much of an opinion of me, and who could blame her?'

'She's never seen you like this,' Nicole pointed out. 'You've been given a wonderful opportunity to prove what you can do and a pretty hardheaded business man like Richard Lindfield, for example, has faith in you. Besides, you're very good with the people you have to deal with—I've seen you. You really listen and you know their problems and you show that you care. Your own experience as an artist has been of enormous help. You actually understand all the technicalities and they're delighted. What about Frances Hallett? You had her eating out of your hand and she very rarely bothers with anyone who can't conduct a reverent and rapturous discussion on fine art.'

'With all due modesty I think she was most interested in *me*, the male!'

'Well, it's no hardship to be good-looking as well,' Nicole laughed. 'How would it be if we asked Chris and Aunt Helen to the opening? Father sees it as a very big affair.'

'I know it's cost a fearful amount of money.'

'You'll get your return,' Nicole said firmly, 'and just think how much you've done yourself. Sleeping here, you probably work until all hours.'

'I do.' Wayne stood up and stretched his tall body. 'Do you think they would come?' he asked abruptly.

'Why not? Chris seems to ask after you more and more these days. Of course I've been deliberately titilating her interest.'

'To what end?' Wayne shot a backward glance at her.

'You care about her, don't you?'

'I really don't think she cares about me!' Wayne said wryly.

'Which is why she's asking so many questions, I suppose?'

'I'm nothing but a damned fool about Chris and I know it,' Wayne answered gloomily. 'You forget she only sees me in comparison with Quinn and her father. Beside either of them I don't rate.'

'Maybe Quinn wouldn't rate in the art world!' Nicole said angrily.

'You're joking!' Wayne turned round to smile at her. 'Darling, you're joking. Talk about Quinn and all that glamour! He carries an aura with him, haven't you noticed? Machismo. He'd fill the biggest gallery with his female admirers alone. He'd even make 'em buy, damn him. No, Nicole, Quinn would be completely successful at anything he tried—and don't forget he's a dagger-sharp business man!'

'He hasn't got your feeling for people,' Nicole persisted, her dark eyes huge.

'He's wounded you, hasn't he?'

'Be sure of it,' Nicole returned more coolly, 'but don't worry, I forgive him. Quinn is a man who's sufficient to himself.'

'I think Margot's finding that out the hard way,' said Wayne. 'She was even talking about taking a trip to Europe the last time I saw her. Quinn's put more staff on Willunga and it's just possible he'll turn the station over to Kim when he marries. Dad might even appreciate it. He lost heart and health when Mother died.'

'Was he terribly upset when you left?' Nicole asked directly.

'No. Worried, I guess. I've never stood on my own two feet before and I never asked him for anything. It was just fortunate Mother left me enough to buy this and get by. I only wish she could be here now to be in on my little triumph—and that's what it's going to be. I'm going to make this work, Nicole. For me, for my partner, for Chris, if she'll ever talk to me, for the family. I've got to show them what I can do.'

'Good for you!' said Nicole in an encouraging voice. 'If you could only talk Polder into the opening exhibition you'd have a runaway success. The critics love him, frequently the public, and you can speak seriously to everyone about buying.'

'At least I could do that with a clear conscience,' Wayne agreed with a faint smile. 'One sees the damnedest kind of horse trading. Tell me,' he brightened and pulled Nicole up by the hand, 'what do you think I should do with that alcove at the top of the stairs?'

*

Six weeks later, Nicole had filled it with an exquisite floral arrangement in the form of a tall triangle that harmonised perfectly with its surroundings. The private showing to be opened by Sir David Harper, the Vice-Chancellor of the University and a personal friend of her father's, was scheduled for six o'clock and over three hundred invitations had been sent out, mostly to known collectors and the moneyed society crowd who at least looked good and guaranteed maximum press coverage. The last time Nicole had spoken to Wayne, at four o'clock, he had sounded almost hysterical, and she thought this had as much to do with the fact that quite a few of the Rossiter clan were flying in as with the usual opening jitters. She had received a telegram from Christine that morning confirming their arrival some little time before six, and they would come straight on to the gallery. After that, they were expected to stay for a few days as Nicole's and her father's guests.

Nicole was frowning at her reflection when her Aunt Sarah put her distinguished head around the door. She was very much like her brother, Nicole's father, tall and dark and smoothly urbane-looking, and she had the kindest heart in the world, as Nicole very well knew.

'Ready, darling?'

Nicole stopped frowning and tried to look gay. 'How do I look?'

'Very smart. Very smart indeed!'

'So do you!' Nicole replied, studying her aunt's tall soignée figure. 'But then you're always that.'

'I try!' Sarah's face flushed very slightly with pleasure. 'Your father's waiting for us downstairs. We're going to pick up Moira on the way.'

'He's getting very fond of her, isn't he?' Nicole commented lightly.

'My darling, I think he'd marry her if marriage ever crossed his mind.'

'Then perhaps we'd better suggest it to him.'

'You wouldn't mind?' Sarah's eyes brooded on her niece's lovely face.

'Good heavens, no!' Nicole protested. 'I'd be delighted. Moira is wonderful with Father. She makes him laugh and relax and she's charming and highly intelligent, and I think she's been very lonely since her husband died. I would never have to pretend to like Moria. I do.'

'And so do I,' Sarah said firmly. 'She's been very gallant, but she needs a good man and a good provider, and thank God your father has always been that.'

'Now it's time he started being kind to himself!' Nicole smiled a little. 'He's been so concerned for me. You both have.'

'But you're all grown up now, darling, aren't you? I mean, you're a woman,' Sarah said quickly. 'Don't think the change in you hasn't gone unnoticed. Whatever happened on Sapphire liberated you from all the old despair. There's a strength in you now, an endurance you can draw on. You went away so nervy and exhausted, almost like a frightened little girl, but you came back with a maturity and resolution both your father and I have noticed. If the showing's a big success tonight, Wayne owes a lot of it to you and Richard.'

'He knows that. About Father, I mean. He's really taken Wayne in hand, and Wayne's worked exceedingly hard. He was incredibly nervous the last time I spoke to him, so we'll have to get there early to lend our support.' Nicole turned back swiftly to the mirror to check her appearance. She was wearing a beautifully cut pale champagne-coloured wool suit with a gold satin shirt and a glitter-sprinkled tie and a dandified little waistcoat. She looked very chic and right up to the minute and her beautiful hair, a little shorter now, was full of body and bounce. 'I suspect it's Chris he's really worried about.'

'And you?'

Across the space of the room Nicole suddenly encountered her aunt's grave, dark glance. 'Don't be silly, Sarah, we won't see Quinn tonight.'

'But you want to?'

'No. If I've given the impression I'm bearing up bravely under a secret passion, I am, but of course Quinn Rossiter doesn't want to marry me or anyone else. I think he'd suffocate under a woman's love.'

Sarah's chiselled mouth softened with compassion. 'Well, darling,' she said gently, 'at least he's succeeded in toughening you up. Peter's selfish passion and his mother's lack of humanity almost brought you to the verge of a breakdown, now you act and you look like a young woman who isn't going to allow herself to be defeated by a bitter experience. Has it ever occurred to you that he may be giving you time to think?'

'About what?' For an instant Nicole's cool reserve broke. 'Quinn's not even human.'

'He's human enough to make you fall madly in love with him—and you have!'

'You should meet him!' Nicole cried almost bitterly, 'you'd fall in love with him yourself. He's fantastic, but make no mistake, he doesn't seem to need anyone. I don't think there's a woman alive splendid enough for him. Wayne's sister tried for years, and she's only one of a long line.'

'All right, pet, don't get emotional. I just have the feeling he's not as "terrible" as you're making out. If you wanted a man to change his whole way of life for you, leave his friends, his family, his environment, wouldn't you want to be sure it was going to work out?'

'Yes,' Nicole gave a little sigh, 'but Quinn has an inbuilt distrust of my kind of woman. The kind to put a man in chains, was how he so nicely put it. I was mad to fall in love with him, but no matter how long I live I'll never regret it.' She looked up and smiled at her aunt with a gentle tenderness that made her eyes look like black velvet. 'I think we'd better go now. In spite of all he's accomplished in these past months Wayne is wretchedly unsure of himself when it comes to his family!'

Less than an hour after the showing was officially opened by Sir David, it was apparent the evening was to be a great success. Swarms of people ringed Polder and Wayne around and the tiny red 'sold' dots decorated all but two frames. These last two paintings were extremely large, but they were already attracting interest from the National Gallery scout.

Wayne was acting the part of entrepreneur to perfection, protective of his budding great artist who was wearing an attractively exhausted air. Nicole, looking across at them, had to smile, then as she turned her head to answer a question with quick eagerness, Christine and Helen came through the doorway, their gazes ranging over the crowd, obviously seeking her out.

'Oh, excuse me!' she said to her small, appreciative audience, and hurried across the room, holding out her hands. 'Aunt Helen, Chris! How lovely to see you!'

'So sorry we're late, dear,' Helen apologised as Nicole brushed her cheek. 'A slight delay with our flight.'

'Everything looks marvellous!' Christine said with genuine appreciation. 'Surely that can't be Wayne holding court over there?'

'He's worked extremely hard,' Nicole answered directly, 'and he's just the right man for this kind of thing. We expect the business to flourish.'

'Who would have believed it!' was all Christine would say, and she stared so hard in Wayne's direction he turned his head and, on seeing her, extricated himself from a group of admirers and came their way.

'Helen. Chris!' Suavely he kissed both women's cheeks. 'I'm so glad you could make it.'

'We're so glad we came, dear,' Helen said affectionately. 'All those lovely red stickers! You must be very pleased?'

'I'll introduce you to Mike in a moment.' Wayne's eyes touched Christine's flushed, pretty face. 'He's going to be one of our really big names. We were extremely fortunate to get him. Of course Richard set it up.'

'And you did the rest!' Nicole maintained firmly.

'Where is your father?' Christine asked, looking about here. 'Oh, there he is over there.' She clasped her hands together almost ecstatically. 'I love the house. It's perfect for a gallery and there's not even a crush with a big showing.'

'Wayne did most of the interior restoration work himself,' Nicole supplied with a sisterly air. 'It looks lovely now, but the house really was in a state of decay when he bought it.'

'Clever boy!' Helen smiled genially, then turned with a look of pleasure as Richard Lindfield approached them, very distinguished and smiling with high good humour. It was an occasion of great amiability and after a few moments he bore Helen off to meet his sister Sarah and their friends, while Wayne took custody of a gracefully willing Christine, promising to introduce her to the artist before making a tour of the exhibition. Quite a few of their relatives were already there and Nicole heard Wayne telling the highly interested Christine that Uncle Hugh had bought one of the best pictures on show.

It seemed to the slightly astonished Nicole that she had been temporarily deserted, without quite knowing how it happened. Her father, always efficient, had carried off Helen and obviously Wayne was employing some cunning tactics of his own. On a station, Wayne had lacked glamour, but he appeared very elegant and charged with energy in his new, far more harmonious milieu. It was a pity he hadn't broken free a lot sooner, Nicole thought, but she had the shrewd suspicion Christine would have no cause for complaint in the future. Wayne was launched on his new career and fulfilment had lent him considerable dignity.

The champagne was flowing freely and it seemed fitting to celebrate, but Nicole had felt nothing but a wild relief when she had learnt that Margot had no intention of flying in for the occasion. Brother and sister, though they bore a close physical resemblance to one another, were actually poles apart in temperament, and Nicole had become genuinely fond of Wayne and pleased and proud of his success. It had never once occurred to her that she had played a major role in Wayne's rehabilitation, but he ever after gave her full credit.

The instant before he touched her shoulder, Nicole knew it was Quinn behind her. Everything in the room fell silent for her except the thin screaming of her violated nerves. She was immensely shocked, and her relaxed body became taut and alert as she spun around and greeted him with cool surprise in spite of her hard pain.

'This *is* a surprise, Quinn!' she exclaimed, and gave him her hand.

'Isn't it?' He bent his dark head and kissed her cheek. He looked taller, darker, more strikingly handsome than ever in a classic British vested sùit, superbly tailored to his lean, wide shouldered frame. She was amazed she could even stand there staring up at him after the frightful way he had treated her, but apparently he had forgotten an awful lot because incredibly he was smiling and his brilliant blue eyes held their usual mocking amusement.

'I've been hearing for months about all the wonderful help you've been giving Wayne, and now at last I can see the results!' He stared about him, head and shoulders over most people.

'I do hope you approve!' she said a little fiercely.

'Oh, I do.' His blue eyes returned to her face. 'Someone had to give Wayne a chance.'

'Well, he couldn't look to the head of the mighty Rossiter clan!' she replied sweetly.

'No, it took our little clear-eyed Nicole. You look very stunning when I thought you might look haggard.'

'On the contrary, I've never felt better. It's all been very stimulating.'

'So I heard from all the heavy correspondence.'

'Isn't it strange Chris didn't tell me you were coming?' she said, still smiling sweetly.

'I thought a surprise would be nicer.'

All of a sudden, the atmosphere was airless and she made a little gesture towards one of the buffet tables. 'Would you like a drink?'

'No. I'd like you to introduce me to your father and aunt.'

'Yes, of course!' A rose flush had risen to her cheeks and she was aware her hands were shaking. People were staring at them, but Nicole knew nothing of their avid interest and cared less. Quinn always brought chaos into her world. It would have been better for her had she fallen in love with the devil himself.

In the end he had to guide her across the room to where her father and Aunt Sarah and Helen were talking cheerfully to a tall, heavily built man Nicole had never seen before. With a cry of delight Helen swooped towards her stepson and held his arm through all the introductions while Matt Rossiter, Wayne's father, regarded Nicole with a certain smiling sombreness, aware that a man might covet her as he never would his own daughter.

Though she had long since ceased to marvel at Quinn and the devastating charm he seemed able to call up on demand, it struck her that he and her father and Aunt Sarah were immediately attracted. Aunt Sarah was gazing up at him with absolute approval and a touch of nostalgia, and her father looked as comfortable with him as if he had known Quinn all his life. It had all happened in a flash and for the rest of the evening Nicole felt she was moving around in a dream world. Probably Quinn would fly back to Sapphire first thing in the morning and she could persuade herself it hadn't really happened. Quinn was a complete mystery to her, but there was no doubt he made an enormous impression on everybody else. Even Wayne looked very touchingly pleased that his cousin, the big cattle baron, had shown up, and besides Quinn had particularly liked the showing and bought the last painting to donate to the new civic centre at Grantham, a fine Outback town dependent upon the big cattle runs and now mining.

No one seemed to be in the least hurry to go home, but Nicole could feel her own little masquerade growing thin. Everyone else might be feeling jovial, but underneath she was a seething mass of agitation that must have been surfacing from Quinn's razor-sharp smile. How dared he come back here and mock her and upset her all over again? She hadn't heard a word from him for long barren months, yet now he was here again, driving her crazy. She was shaking with resentment when she should have been meekly accepting his arrogant, thick-skinned ways. What were a few kisses after all? He was too smart to do anything dreadfully indiscreet or binding, though she remembered with savage clarity how close he had come to full arousal.

When Christine made the brilliant suggestion that they

go on to the Top of the Town to catch the Silver Convention Quinn declined, saying in his customary high-handed fashion that he and Nicole had so much to discuss he intended taking her somewhere a lot quieter. He might have planned it, for no one came to her rescue, indeed they stood back smiling as though they enjoyed this piece of news.

'Take my car,' Richard Lindfield offered affably, his smile broadening.

'Thank you, but I've hired one until I leave.' Quinn returned the smile. 'Say goodnight, Nicole. You can hear all about the floor show in the morning.'

'This has been one of the most enjoyable evenings of my life,' Aunt Sarah commented, almost immediately.

'And it's not over yet!' Matt Rossiter's rather tired eyes had brightened considerably. 'Tell me, what the devil is the Silver Convention?'

'Better ring to see if we can get in.' Christine drew closer to Wayne.

'We will.' Richard Lindfield informed her. 'It's not fair, I know, but I have a friend in the head waiter. Frankly, Matt, I don't know much about the group, but they tell me they're terrific entertainers.'

'Then it's settled.' Quinn took a firm hold of Nicole's arm. 'I'll see you all again very soon.'

'I believe you will!' Richard Lindfield shook hands with the younger man. 'I believe you will!'

Nicole went dazedly, convinced she was being out-manoeuvred by the lot of them, a strategy planned in advance. Even when they were driving swiftly away from the gallery, she sat almost numbly. Quinn didn't seem inclined to talk either, so finally she turned her head and asked expressionlessly:

'Where are we going?'

'Back to my hotel. It's been one hell of a day.'

'*I'm* not!'

'You're not what?' Very briefly he glanced at her.

'Coming back to your hotel.'

'Don't think for a moment I'm going to try to talk to you in the car.'

This made her give a little choking laugh. 'About what? I've wasted too much time on you already!'

'How so?' he asked deliberately. 'Drastic methods are cruel, I know, but sometimes they're necessary.'

'Are you trying to reassure me?' Her tone sounded outraged and she tried to get a hold on herself. 'Listen, Quinn,' she continued more calmly, 'we've got nothing to talk about.'

'Then why did you come?'

'As it happened, it was more like being kidnapped.'

'You can't forgive me?' His mouth twisted ironically.

'I'm all grown up now, Quinn. Meeting you was one heck of an experience, but I'm over it now.'

'Congratulations!' he said dryly.

'When do you go back to Sapphire?' she asked, gazing ahead intently.

'In a day or so. I never like to be away long.'

'No!' she gave a funny little laugh. 'First of all, above everything, you're the cattle baron, a powerful person in your world.'

'I told you a long time ago what Sapphire meant to me,' he said tautly.

'It's all right.' Nicole looked down at her clenched hands. 'I understand. I really do.'

'Did you think I wanted to hurt you deliberately?' He glanced at her briefly and his eyes glittered in the faint light.

'Believe me, I know you wouldn't hesitate!' Her mouth trembled and she could hardly stop herself from bursting into tears. He really was so terribly cruel, and she loved him in spite of everything.

'Yet you don't appear to have been suffering,' he

pointed out dryly. 'Whatever your little grief you seem to have put it out of your mind.'

'Then I've learned something, haven't I?'

'Let's drink to that!'

For the next few minutes all his attention was focused on parking the car in the illuminated grounds of the hotel. There was no one in the foyer except the receptionist who had her fair head bent away from them, absorbed in some papers in her hand, neither was there anyone in the elevator.

On the top floor Quinn guided Nicole along to his room and she went, though her face looked enchantingly moody. When he switched on the light she stood where she was, motionless, looking around the hotel's most luxurious accommodation. He obviously liked to live like a prince, with a prince's privileges, wherever he went.

'You don't limit yourself to anything less than the best, do you?' she said steadily.

'As it happens I sleep just as well under the stars.' He walked over to the bar and leisurely poured himself a drink. 'Would you like anything?'

'This isn't the seduction scene, is it?'

'Perhaps we can talk about it a few years from now.'

'How's Margot?' she asked sweetly, and sank down into the cushiony banquette seating that half lined one wall.

'Why don't you come right out with what you're trying to say?'

Instead of taking the armchair opposite her, Quinn sat beside her and passed her a glass of champagne. 'I don't like to be too blatant!' she said, taking it.

'You were stupid to think I had any interest in Margot.'

'Whatever you say. Personally I thought she'd make an admirable wife.'

'Didn't it occur to you that I was waiting far too long? I've known Margot all my life.'

'Then what did you do to make her fall in love with you?' She took a sip of her drink, then put it away.

'It's Margot's nature to want the unobtainable. In any case, I disclaim any responsibility in the matter.'

'Did she ever give you the file?' she asked.

'I've forgotten.'

'Tell me!' Despite herself she turned on him and he moved swiftly, his arms beneath her, lifting her right into his arms.

'Are you ever going to be free of your past?' He bent his head and found her mouth, controlling her easily, until the rigidity of her body gave way to a tremulous yielding, like a statue coming to life, and her mouth breathed words into his own.

'Oh, go away, Quinn!' she murmured. 'For God's sake leave me alone. I can't bear it.'

'Why not?' He drew her even closer, looking into her eyes.

'I'm not like you!' she said passionately, exalted by the sense of wrong that was being done to her. 'I can't turn if off and on at will!'

'And I can?' His blue eyes were blazing at her, devouring her face so she felt her breath shorten and a voice within her protested that the expression on his face was surely that of a lover.

'Have you really forgotten? It's six months!'

'Six months, one week and four days!'

'Surely you're not trying to pay me back for something?' she cried out, exasperated.

'Oh, don't be absurd!' He kissed her again with a deep hunger so her resistance merged into a revealing surrender. Every time he touched her she felt drugged and trancelike, unable to fight out of such smothering desire.

'You hated me. You know you did!'

'Did I ever say so?' He lifted his head and gave a little bitter smile. 'You're a woman, you've got a woman's instincts. You must know how it's been for me since the first moment I saw you. I've wanted you against all my will, against a certainty I'd be making a great error in judgment, but even that didn't matter. All these long months without you I'd have given anything to hear your young voice and your laughter, to see your beautiful innocent face, the perfect, natural way you ride. I've been alone, quite alone, and your pull has been relentless.'

'Yet you confess it openly?' Almost shyly, she held her hand against the hard, beautiful bones of his face. 'What does it mean, Quinn? Please tell me.'

'It means I love you,' he said quietly, but with some deep eddy of emotion that had the power to turn her heart over. 'It means whether it's good or bad for you, I'll never let you go. The price you'll have to pay for marrying me, I suppose.' Gently he curled a gleaming strand of her hair around his hand and pulled on it. 'You'll never be free of me, Nicole.'

'Do you think I would ever want to be?' she asked, in a soft, shaken voice. There were tears in the brilliant darkness of her eyes. 'See, you have me now. So long as you love me, there's nothing you could do to make me leave you, nothing to make you afraid. You're the only ecstasy I've ever known in my life, my beloved, though you've been excessively cruel to me.'

'To myself!' he whispered, and kissed her mouth again. 'It was too long and it drove me mad, but I had to be sure. I had to give you time to get over your memories, to collect yourself. You know what marriage to me means.'

'Yes, heaven!' Nicole said intensely. 'I was so terrified you would hate me for what happened to Peter.'

'Then you must have a strange opinion of me!' He held her trembling body and smoothed her hair from her face. 'Be quiet a little, darling. You must learn to see things with some sense of proportion. You weren't responsible for that young man's death; he made it happen himself. Too many mistakes happen on our roads, too many taken chances that end in tragedy. Man must have a reverence for life. I don't want to hurt you and it must have worried your father, but the young man you allowed yourself to become engaged to didn't have a great deal of character. That much I've found out.'

'But I found out myself!' she protested pleadingly.

'Of course! You're very young, very sensitive. The whole incident naturally shocked you and other people can make things so very unpleasant. But it's all over now. Nothing bad will ever happen to you again. I swear it!'

His eyes, so blue and intense, sparkled deeply, and Nicole could see herself reflected in their brilliant depths. With a little moan of wonder she lifted her arms and encircled his neck. 'Darling, you're here with me,' she whispered ardently. 'I've been so lonely!'

'Then show me!'

There was urgency and naked longing on his face, a storm of passion barely held under restraint. His hand shaped her nape beneath the heavy silken thickness of her hair and she twisted nearer so the soft weight of her body was full against him, her eyes closing, her mouth parting on a soft breath of rapture:

'I will, I promise, for the rest of my life!'

Harlequin Omnibus

THREE love stories in ONE beautiful volume

The joys of being in love...
the wonder of romance...
the happiness that true love brings...

Now yours in the HARLEQUIN OMNIBUS
edition every month wherever
paperbacks are sold.